STOLEN

TRIBES, #2

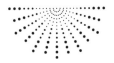

MILANA JACKS

PROLOGUE

TRIBES SERIES QUICK REFERENCE

Tribes series takes place on a planet called Nomra Prime. Thus far, we have the Ka and the Ra tribe that signed a peace treaty after eons of wars. On both sides, females and young are almost nonexistent, and the Ka males are near extinction.

Their alien classification is *Predator*. They're dual-form aliens. Their hunting form is a hunter and often stands as tall as a horse with exposed large sharp teeth, meaning the hunter's lips don't cover the teeth. They have large erect ears, which make them appear bigger and more frightening. They're extremely fit and agile, and can execute leaps we (humans) consider impossible.

Most tribes can be united under a single "King" they designate by adding -i to the tribe name. So for Ka tribe, it's Kai where -i at the end indicates a male who is a leader of the Ka tribe, the top of their food chain and this male always eats first.

Inside a single tribe, an earl governs a smaller territory called an earldom. There can be many many earldoms in any one tribe.

Portal: a spatial shortcut to another place on the planet. A closed portal, meaning a vertical golden line, is not visible to the human eye.

Main Characters:

Hart : Ka tribal leader, Alpha of the Ka tribe. His designation is Kai.

Stephanie: Hart's human. Believed to be Amti.

Nar: Hart's brother and second strongest of the Ka males.

Michelle: Nar's human.

Mas: Ka tribe portal genius.

Tis: Mas's brother.

Ark: Ra tribe's Alpha, meaning the strongest of the Ra males but not an elected leader, meaning the Ra do not have a single "King" named Rai where -i at the end indicates his "kingship" over other tribal members. Hart's frenemy.

Sha-male: a male who performs religious rites, sacrifices, prayers (priest, imam, etc)

Gur: Earl in the Ra tribe. Wants war.

Feli: Second to Gur in Gur's earldom.

The Lore: Tribes worship the female. Goddesses are admired, feared, and respected. Goddess are believed to be returning as human females so that they may walk the lands again.

Bera: Goddess of fertility.

Aimea: Goddess of doom. Most feared.

Herea: Goddess of hunt and harmony. Most popular.

Amti: Goddess of madness and lust.

Aoa: Goddess of thunder and pain. Patron goddess of the Ka tribe.

Mae: Goddess of fire and lies. Aoa's mother.

Locations:

Kalia: Ka tribe capital. Near the Ra border. Suffered extensive structural damage during the wars.

TBA as the series rolls ...

CHAPTER ONE

NAR

Lightning cracks the sky, and the coming storm gathers the dark clouds as hundreds of predators assemble on the open field. The mud makes the already soft ground softer, and my boots sink lower. I lift a foot and move closer to Mas. Leaning in, I whisper. "How many are entering the games?"

"Two hundred at most." He gives me a knowing look.

The prize is a womankind who crash-landed in the Ra tribe territory. Neither the Ra nor my tribe, the Ka, have competed for a female in a decade, the games my brother recently held notwithstanding. After the wars between the Ka and Ra, my tribe was left with no females or young. Sterility plagues the Ra females, so they've got nothing too. There're over four hundred males in the camp and more in the nearby village, so why are only two hundred entering?

Mas and I know Earl Gur plans to break the truce that Ark, his tribal Alpha, signed with my brother, Hart, and that's why I'm here. To kill Gur in the games.

"Have you seen Gur?" I ask.

Mas shakes his head.

"Are any of our males here?"

"As far as I can see, only us."

A male bumps my shoulder, and I grunt from the impact. He walks on as if he didn't do it on purpose. Old wounds die hard, and the animosity between the two tribes goes back centuries. We've fought this tribe for either land or revenge, and sometimes for no reason at all.

"That's Feli, Gur's new second."

I killed the old second. "You think Gur's holding a grudge against me?" I ask. A rhetorical question. Every one of the Ra holds a grudge against the Ka, especially against me. I've slaughtered many of them on open fields like this one. That's why Mas and I stand alone and to the left of the wooden stage platform with a single chair that I presume the prize will sit upon as she awaits the games. "I wonder what she looks like," I say.

Mas side-eyes me, lifts a foot, and moves back a bit. I step back beside him. We're gonna sink in the mud to our knees if we wait any longer. A drop of rain hits my nose, and I turn up my face and squint. The sky's all but black.

"This should be fun," Mas says, face tilted up as well.

Competing on this muddy terrain while it's raining, and the clouds signaling a thunderstorm as well? Yeah, should be fun. The two-hundred-and-some males shuffle. Whispers and hooting sound as Feli takes to the stage, his boots smearing mud all over it.

"Here we go," Mas says and cracks his neck. Portals are the way we travel across the land, and Mas gets off on being the finest portal master in the lands. Anyone who takes up portal controls during the games is his target. Not to kill, though Mas has no issues with eliminating males, but more to wrestle portal control from the one who's running it.

Before pulling up the portal controls, a series of holographs that Feli will monitor during the games, Feli glances at Mas and smirks, swiping his hand over the control panel.

Screens pop up all around him, showing us the terrain Feli designed for the games. I recognize some local places here in the village, others in the middle of nowhere inside Ra territory, and one that looks familiar, as if it's one of our villages in the south.

"Is that what I think it is?" I ask Mas. If it is one of our villages, then Feli is telling us he has a portal hidden inside our territory.

"Possibly, but I can't be sure. I gotta get in there." Feli might have breached a territory inside Ka land, one that contains Mas's portal controls. While we all have entry points into each other's territories, we keep them secret so that our spies can move safely in and out of enemy land.

"It could be a trap, Mas."

"I know, but I have to check it out anyway."

"You could get stuck in there for spans on end." If it's an illusion, a replica of our land to lure Mas and me into it, we'd get stuck inside a dead-end portal leading nowhere. Such illusions are hard to breach and could prove deadly if there's no way out.

"Don't worry about me. Worry about Gur."

"Yeah, well, he's not here, and separating us works to their advantage."

Mas presses a claw over his lips and taps them. "Where's the prize?"

I shrug as if I don't care while my fingers itch to reach into my pocket and pull out the prize's underpants, a piece of red cloth that hides the place between her legs. The scent has faded since I first found it, so I can't wait to sniff straight from the source. Just thinking about the smell makes me hard.

I adjust my erection.

7

Mas taps his nose, telling me he can smell I'm hard, and no amount of lying would convince him otherwise. Our Kai, the alpha of my tribe and my brother, sent me to kill Gur. If I can secure the prize, the womankind, in the process, that's great. But if I can't, Gur takes priority over the games. I should be worrying about where Gur is and not when I'll get to see the prize and how I'm gonna sniff between her legs.

"One hundred ninety-two males entered. Closing the games in..." Feli lifts a hand and counts. "Five, four, three..." I search for Gur.

"He's not entering," Mas says.

"Fuck." The games get deadly out there. It would be easy to eliminate Gur. Out here, killing a Ra earl could incite another conflict. If he won't enter, killing him with nobody seeing me do it becomes almost impossible.

Feli closes the entries to the games, and the bitchhole Ra cheer. Pissed, Mas and I growl low in our chests. We expected Gur to enter. An Earl usually enters even when he doesn't want the prize. It's a show of support for his people and makes for fantastic competition because everyone wants to beat up their superior for fun and games. Normally, you couldn't beat up an earl, or a Kai, in our case, or he'd kill you. That's why the games are fun. They always have been and always should be. But over the turns, our people and the Ra alike have grown so bloodthirsty that we don't know what fun means anymore.

A few spans ago, even my brother killed our own males during our games. It set a bad precedent, but I trust he did it because they left him no choice. I heard those males were protesting because he admitted a Ra tribal alpha into our games. It rubbed some of our males all wrong, and a subtribe formed, intent on killing my brother.

During our last war, Ark, the Ra tribal Alpha, killed more

8

of our males than I have of his, and that's saying something. Despite that, my brother let him compete and even let him win.

Rain pelts the weapons strapped around my waist, drops hitting the hilt of my dagger and ringing in my ears. I rest a hand on the hilt and wipe water off my face. It accumulates again, and I shake my head, annoyed I'm getting wet. Mas secures his hair at the back of his head and shakes off his body. We're predators, hunters, and we dislike standing in the rain.

The Ra males start growling.

Everyone's getting irritated because Gur's taking forever to bring out the prize. It's on purpose, I'm sure, to get us all worked up and agitated. If he's not competing, then he's watching the games and monitoring with Feli, sitting right near the prize, guarding her so nobody steals her. I snort. As if any male would stoop so low as to steal a prize instead of winning her fair and square.

Between the grunts and growls, I hear the males on the other side of the podium cheering, so something's coming. The crowd parts, revealing a moving green feather. Gur's easy to spot as he's always got this green decoration on top of his head. He thinks his mother was descended from Herea, goddess of the hunt, so he wears the bird's feathers.

Gur climbs the platform, wheezing a bit over his bulging gut. He's been eating well, slowing down. He couldn't compete even if he wanted to. Fitness is everything in the games, and the female will take notice of mine. Naturally. I'm fucking fit.

"Where's the girl?" I growl, then stare, needing no answer because Gur's climbing up the stage holding a leash attached to a female who's crawling behind him.

Silence falls over the camp. Even Mas adjusts his erection.

A female on a leash teases our darkest fantasies, the ones I believe every male in the lands harbors since a very young age. We just haven't ever seen it play out in front of our eyes.

"Don't even think about competing for real," I hiss into Mas's ear.

He purses his lips, eyes twinkling with lust.

"I mean it."

"Quiet while I work out what I'm seeing. I can't believe he brought her out this way. It's so wrong."

"They're gonna want her bad."

"More reason for you to figure out how to kill Gur now and not compete at all."

"Yeah, let me just arrowhead him from here and walk away."

Mas chuckles.

We are so fucked. And not only because Gur is practically unkillable now. Ever since I found the underpants, I knew I wanted to sniff where the smell came from again. It's a breeding instinct, nothing more, nothing less. And I expected the same sort of female as my brother's female. But this one is smaller, thinner, with long black hair that's dragging in the mud left from Feli's boots over the platform. She's wearing blue pants like my brother's female, and a white shirt.

As she climbs the chair and sits with her head down, instinctively I move toward her. Mas grabs my wrist. Turning toward Mas, I snarl when Feli shouts, "The prize!"

His shout breaks through some of the fantasy fog in my brain and brings me back to reality where we are two males against two hundred, not to mention the other two hundred spread out between the camp and the village.

"We need to stay alive," Mas hisses, then releases my wrist. "Get it together."

I roll my shoulders and return to my place beside him. "Maybe she's ugly."

He snorts.

Yeah. If she's anything like my brother's mate—small, cute, submissive, with round colored eyes and a perky nose—I'm fucked. Huddled in on herself, wet black hair shielding her face, she rubs her arms, looking lost and alone on a chair large enough to fit a grown hunter. Gur tucks a claw under her chin and forces her to lift her face. She slaps his hand away and leans as far as she can away from him. Which isn't very far.

He tries again, and she leans away more. At this rate, she'll fall off the chair. Gur grabs her by the throat and moves her hair away from her face, then steps back.

Pale face. Small nose. Pretty plush lips, colored blue-gray unlike red as I've seen on other humans. Slanted eyes with black irises in stark contrast to the white around them.

"Real ugly," Mas says.

"Mm-hm." I give him a side-eye, and sure enough, Mas is staring at her.

"You can't compete for real," I tell him.

"Neither can you," he reminds me. "Make it look good, but you're here for Gur's blood."

"I'm fine."

He glances at me and grunts.

The female turns her head, and we lock gazes. The world vanishes, and my heart beats loudly. I hear it in my ears. My hunter, as if waking up, takes notice of the female, stirring my bones, making my muscles relax.

Mas slaps the back of my head.

I wince and slap him back.

He points to his eyes. "Eyes off the prize, hooker." Hooker is a derogatory term for a male who releases a hook and marks a female. A selfish male who wants a female only for himself. Both my father and brother are hookers. I'm no hooker. Just because I find her attractive and pitiable on that

11

platform doesn't mean I'm gonna compete in the games. And it definitely doesn't mean I'm gonna mark her.

CHAPTER TWO

MICHELLE

D renched, cold, and led on a leash onto a wooden podium in the pouring rain, I sit on an icy, hard wooden chair, taking stock of the aliens who hold me captive, grateful that Feli, my keeper, finally dragged me out of the hole in the ground Gur kept me in for days. Or maybe weeks. I don't know how long it's been since I crashed on this planet on my way to Joylius, where I would have swum in the ocean with cute little sea creatures. I'm swimming in tears now.

Eyes still adjusting to the daylight, I blink several times, trying to see better, but the rain pelts my face and makes it hard to see. I rub my shoulders and pull up my feet to keep my body from freezing. Jeans and a thin white shirt won't do in this weather. If I stay like this, I'll get hypothermia. Maybe that's a good thing. I don't know why they've gathered or what's going on, but when he pulled me out of the hole, Feli installed a translator, so I'll find out.

Lifting the hem of my soaked shirt, I wipe my face, take stock of the males. There's a lot of them. A sea of pale eyes, golden beads, and other nice accessories woven into long thick hair. They wear furs and kilts and carry prehistoric weapons. If I hadn't been kept underground and treated like an animal, I might admire these space Vikings. However, they chose to treat me worse than my brother did on a bad day and lock me up underground, where I wondered if the small, double-chinned, hairless animals scurrying along the hole's walls would eat my toes while I slept.

I hate them all. The aliens and the animals on this planet.

Gur tugs on my leash, and I grip the leather with a hand so he doesn't break my neck. He grabs my jaw and forces me to look up into his pale eyes.

"As you can all see," he says through my translator, "the female is healthy, with breasts that can produce milk to feed the young. She has a womb and is a carnivore."

The males cheer.

I swallow, fear making me sick. I feel like vomiting. I was better off with no translator and forgotten down the hole.

"It has been said our neighbors," Gur continues, but pauses when the males boo. He chuckles and raises his hand for silence. "It has been said the Ka tribal leader competed in the games for a female just like her. He lost to our Alpha."

They cheer again. "Where is Ark?" someone asks.

Gur shrugs and walks to Feli, who's been watching something in front of him the entire time. As Gur nears him, Feli's expression shows displeasure, and I look away, my gaze landing far to the left, where two males stand alone, clearly away from the others. I rest my chin on my knee and rub my arms again, staring at the two males. The tribal markings on their faces, the way they braided and styled their hair away from their faces more on the top than the sides, as well as their clothes, makes me think they're outsiders. Their black leather kilts are made of several pieces stitched together, and they're not wearing elaborately decorated belts over their middles like Gur's males, just a single black belt that's used to hold their weapons.

The male with lighter hair whispers into the ear of the one with darker hair, who's watching me, a small smirk lifting the corner of his lips. He reaches into his pocket and pulls out something, holds it between his claws for a few seconds, then slips it back into his pocket. He mouths a few words as if trying to talk to me, but I can't understand. Whatever he's trying to say can't be good, so fuck him too. He's like all the others, even if he isn't dressed like them.

Feli blocks my view, and when I look up, he reaches out and moves stray hairs away from my face.

"I will win," he says.

"Win what?"

"The games."

"Good for you." Maybe Gur brought me here to watch a spectacle. Maybe they're gladiators and not Vikings. Lord knows I have no idea where I landed or what's going to happen to me. All I know is that I woke up inside a hole with a wooden door above me, through which I barely heard anything. For days, there was nothing but me and four wet walls about fifty feet underground.

"You're not competing." Gur walks by Feli and sits next to me, then takes my hand in his. I yank my hand back. He grabs my wrist and snarls. His upper lip peels back, showing long sharp canines. When he takes my hand again, I recoil but don't protest.

Feli growls. "I am competing."

Gur strokes the top of my hand. "Since you've guarded her so well thus far, you're the guardian for the games."

"I have entered the games," Feli grits out.

"Un-enter."

Feli bends at the waist so his face is inches from Gur's. "You can't ban me. All males can compete and are equal in the games."

A growl from Gur's chest is unlike anything I've ever heard. He releases my hand as Feli leans closer, their noses almost touching. Both males are growling, their upper lips twitching, and then their jaws drop, and the cheekbones move in a...an inhuman way. Slowly, I withdraw my hand from Gur's and put my feet on the platform. I stand and move my chair away from them. Since Gur holds my leash, I end up only few feet away, but that's better than right next to him.

"Psst," sounds, and I snap my head in the direction of the pair of males, who've moved to the front. The one with darker hair holds something in his palm. I think he's trying to show me what it is, and I glance at Gur first to check if he's looking. He's arguing with Feli, so I lean in a bit, trying to make out what the dark-haired male is holding. I shake my head. No idea what it is, and why is he trying to show me anything anyhow? Why would I care? He's one of them.

I lean back and curl up on the chair again.

The male rolls his eyes so dramatically, he does a circle with his head.

Feli walks back to where he's been standing the entire time, poking things in the air before him, things I can't see but can tell they're there. He appears displeased. I don't believe he's competing.

Gur walks to me and strokes my cheek. I want to recoil again, but don't. If I behave like a snarling, snapping idiot, he'll starve me and beat me, so no, thanks. Calm and cool like this, I might actually survive this ordeal until my brother comes for me.

He's *the man* over at National Security, and I'm sure he

won't stop looking when I don't return from my vacation. Hell, he might even already be looking since I didn't call him when I arrived. It has been a terrible ordeal, but I haven't lost hope yet and will keep myself alive until he finds me.

"Two hundred males," Gur announces, and the crowds cheer. The two in the front shout along with them, so they're all the same after all.

"Three days," Gur says, and the two in the front pull something like charcoal from their pockets.

"Two nights," Feli says.

The charcoal melts in their palms, and they draw lines on their faces, making me think of war paint. The one with dark hair flicks the paint in his palm. It splatters over my face. I flinch and wipe it off, smearing it all over my hands and white shirt. Like I needed more humiliating. *Fuck you,* I mouth.

He smiles.

Asshole.

"One winner," Feli says as Gur pulls my chair back to him, bending to see the black stain over my jeans. I am so offended that the male has thrown something at me. It feels like a rotten tomato in my face. Humiliated, I want to cry, and my eyes fill with tears.

A piercing whistle rings in my ears and draws me back out of my self-pity party. Males snarl and sprint across the muddy open field. A bolt of lightning strikes in the distance and thunder roars over the shouting males seconds later. The sky darkens, and rain pours harder, and I can barely make out what I'm seeing. Pockets of different landscape pop up everywhere, males leaping into them, then disappearing as if they never existed. In a matter of seconds, the field empties. I look to Feli for an explanation, but he's staring into space and moving his hands in front of him.

Gur shifts in his seat. "Female," he says.

That's me. "Yes, sir."

"Good. The translator works."

I nod again, eager to hear what he has to say. He turns to me, his jawbone kind of moving in an unnatural, scary-as-fuck way. I want to recoil again, but gather strength and ball my fists. Faced with his pale gaze, I swallow.

"When the males return with gifts, you will not accept a gift from either of the two Ka males."

"Two Ka males?"

"The other tribe," Feli says, glancing back at me as if that clarifies everything.

Gur stands and brushes his thumb over my cheek. "If I were younger, I'd have competed for you, but alas, I'm too old now."

Feli snorts, and Gur snaps his head Feli's way. "Tread carefully, my boy."

Feli continues moving his arms, agile fingers swiping back and forth. I'm dying of curiosity about what he's doing, but the tension between my captors is high, so I ask nothing, biding my time and thinking that when I faint from hypothermia and fall from the chair, they'll have to keep me somewhere warmer or maybe even return me into the hole. At least there, I'll be alone in my misery.

My teeth chatter.

The rain keeps pouring, soaking my hair and clothes.

"She will die if you keep her here for the span," Feli says.

Gur snorts. "Maybe you want to keep her warm until the night?"

Feli's jaw works while Gur laughs, and something he said replays in my mind. I clear my throat. "What did you mean when you said you'd have competed for me?"

Gur claps. "So she speaks!"

I speak, asshole. I'm not an animal. You are. "Yes, sir."

18

"The males have three days and two nights to court you. They rack up points as they search for gifts for you. The winner takes the prize. Don't forget what I said." He points at the Ka males lingering in the distance now, just standing there, observing. "Those two, you will ignore."

CHAPTER THREE

NAR

As I stand in place, my boots sinking deeper and deeper into the mud, I can't take my eyes off the female. If I don't move, the ground will swallow me. I step forward, and Mas walks away, likely thinking I'm gonna follow him according to the plan we contrived before entering the games.

But Mas doesn't know I know what this little female smells like, and that, deep down inside, I didn't come here for Gur. I came here for her, and I'm gonna get her. I move toward her again when Mas appears in front of me, his hunter lurking behind his pale eyes. Bright orange eyes flash at me. "What the fuck are you thinking?" Mas whisper-hisses.

I'm thinking about snatching her. "You said Gur would enter the games," I tell him. Mas erected a secret portal inside Ra territory, one that can take us in and out of here if we need a quick exit, and we're gonna need it if events don't go as planned, meaning if the Ra figure out we're here to kill Gur, their earl. Things are already looking shitty for us, and definitely not going as planned. Gur was supposed to enter the games. I was gonna off him during the games while also winning, thereby securing myself a breeder. "Why is he still in the camp?"

Mas looks around, then steps closer, his chest bumping mine. He whispers, "Gur entered, then exited at the last second before Feli closed the games. We proceed and play until we have a better chance at targeting him."

I grunt, moving back because his proximity and his dominant hunter irritates my hunter. I'm already irritated with the scene I witnessed here. The rain is pelting her body, and she's shaking from the cold. She looks like an abandoned pup instead of a prized breeder, one of only two my tribe has competed for in over a decade.

Mas narrows his eyes. "What just went through your head?"

"I'm gonna snatch her."

His eyes widen, and he grabs my biceps, digging his claws into my skin. A growl rises from my chest, and he matches it with his own, pounding me with his dominance, trying to get me to fold. "We cannot go to war. Our Kai and your brother ordered an assignation to prevent a war. If you snatch the prize, you're on your own. Nobody will host you, not even your brother."

My jawbone rises and falls, and I hate Mas for his logic and forecasting of my grim future if I run up there and throw her over my shoulder, then make a run for it. Even if I escape the territory while carrying the most prized possession in the lands, I'd have to take her far away and live in hiding for the rest of our lives, if only to spare my tribe the Ra slaughter. Yet again. Snatching her would devastate my brother. "Mas, I can't leave her here to get sick and die."

"She's not your concern. We're not here for her."

His eyes widen more, and I wanna laugh.

"I smelled her, and the hunter latched on," I tell him.

Mas shakes his head. "Unlatch him."

"No can do."

A whine escapes Mas's throat, and he closes his eyes, breathes in, then out. "Fine, Nar. We will compete as a team. I'll do everything I can to help you win. Meanwhile, you'll also do everything you can to execute the thing we came here for. But you will not snatch her. I can't help you if you do."

I nod.

"Good." He pats my head. "Good. Let's get moving, then."

I nod and unlace the fur that covers my back. It's the fur from Jeh, a Ra I skinned after we retook one of our villages from his subtribe. I wore it for Gur so he would remember that span, and I wore it so that his people would recognize Jeh's pelt. It's a unique pattern native to the Ra living in the western parts. Their hunters are incredibly hard to kill when fighting hunter vs male. I fought him on two legs and strangled him with my own hands. His pelt is my most prized trophy.

"What are you doing?" Mas whines.

"Stop freaking out and watch."

"Fuck me," he says. "I said I don't want to go, but Hart made me go. He made me go because he knew you'd latch onto the female. He knew, didn't he?"

"He knew."

"I hate you. I hate you hard."

I blow him a kiss because Mas can be really dramatic and doesn't hate me. He looks out for me like my own brother. Even more than my brother.

I move around him, a Ra pelt draped over my forearm.

Gur stands. Feli stops handling the portals and approaches the female. When he sees I'm gunning straight for the female, he steps in front of her as if to protect her. At the platform, I grind my teeth and lock eyes with him. "I have brought a gift. Fuck off so she may see it."

He crosses his arms over his chest. "You didn't compete."

"I don't have to. You made it easy."

He snorts. "Pussy."

A wave of anger washes over me. "Come here, puppy, and I'll make you my bitch."

"The female must see all the gifts and choose," Mas says. "You know the rules."

Gur strokes his beard and nods, then sits back down, but the little hookhole, Feli, still stands in front of the female. Does he want me to move him? I fist my hand, claws digging into my skin, cutting, making me bleed. If I step up to the platform with no invitation from her, I forfeit today, making my win unlikely.

I smile. They do want me to step up. They want to provoke me, so I can't give them the pleasure.

Behind Feli, small bare feet touch the slippery wet floor. The female walks around Feli and stands before me. Raindrops bounce off the top of her head and run down her cheeks, soaking her completely. Her lips aren't red. They're purple. Her dark, almost black eyes are slanted in the corners, but wide and expressive. My sad puppy.

"I brought you fur," I say in my most love-bug voice. "It will keep you warm."

She's blinking away the rain and wipes her face, then looks to Gur as if seeking guidance.

"If you wanna get out of here, I'm your pass," I say.

Gur snorts. "You don't protect your females. The entire world knows that about the Ka."

I ignore him. It is true. We marched into Ra lands, leaving our villages and towns unprotected, and they came and slaughtered everyone. Not only that, they occupied our lands for many turns before Hart and I grew strong enough to lead

23

the Ka tribe and regain the lands. We still have some territory under Ra occupation, but Hart signed the truce
regardless.

"If you accept the fur," Feli says, "this Ka wins a night with
you. Think about what a night with him would be like and
decide."

I snort. "Female, a night with me will be warm and pleasant. I will feed you a chunk of my own flesh."

Her brow furrows. She appears confused.

"Or soup?" I prompt. "Mas can make soup, can't you,
Mas?" When Mas doesn't answer, I nudge him.

"Yes," he says.

Mas hunts for fresh meals like all the males, so we don't
know how to make anything. Mas probably has no idea what
soup is, but I do, because Hart briefed me on all things I
should know about womankind: Smells good. Looks cute.
Eats predators. May be a goddess.

"Chicken soup," I press onward, having no clue what that
means. But she does. Oh yes, she does. Her eyes light up, and
a small smile plays on her lips. She walks down the steps and
turns her back to me, then stands there.

What? What is she doing?

I look to Mas for help.

"Go on," he says and motions with his hand.

Go on what? I can't ask and appear as if I don't know,
when he clearly knows things I should know.

"Put the pelt over her shoulders," he says, practically
spelling out the words. "Keep the female warm. It's a fine
courting gesture."

Oh fuck. I'd never have guessed. In games, we drop the
gifts on the steps of the platform. We don't hand them to the
female directly, but this is a womankind, and I'm learning. I
shake out the rain from the pelt, put it over her shoulders,

bundle her up, then spin her around. I wipe water off her face and move her hair out of the way.

She looks up at me and says, "Winner, winner, chicken dinner."

I think I'm the chicken. She wants a chunk of me.

CHAPTER FOUR

MICHELLE

U nlike the others, this male offered me a pelt, a furry, warm pelt, and bundled me up. I don't care about their games or which male is going to bring me what. This one offered kindness and a cup of chicken soup for dinner. Gur asked me not to accept, but I'd be pretty stupid to refuse it. After a few hours in this weather, I'd have died. Besides, this male and Gur sound like enemies, and the enemy of my enemy is my friend.

Whether this male will deliver on the soup or not is all the same to me. If I go back to the hole where Gur kept me, I'm not getting soup for dinner. Provided I make it through the night, which I won't.

Vicious weather.

Vicious aliens.

Vicious fate I've succumbed to, but I want to live, and he offered me a better chance of survival against the elements.

We stand there facing each other, and I'm taking in his face while he fastens the pelt over me, fixes it so it covers my head. His jawbone has edges, and it's made harder with tattoos aesthetically drawn to show off the hard edges. He's made himself appear scary and fierce.

"Are you a warrior around here?" I ask.

"Not around here."

"But you are classified as a warrior?"

"Yes."

"You all are warriors, then?"

He tugs on the last leather string around my throat, then bends to secure my legs. I dip my head to see what he's doing. He takes off another pelt from his back, this one thinner and hairless, almost like a sleeveless coat.

He looks up and smiles. "I love seeing my female wrapped in my kill." He tightens up the pelt and rises. "All done now," he announces, then picks me up and throws me over his shoulder like a sack of potatoes. As he marches away, I try to lift my head to see the platform, but all I see is the pelt secured over my head. Giving up seeing anything, and with my hands and feet tied, I bounce off his hard back. From the corner of my eye, I see another pair of boots walking along with us.

"She's not your female," the other male with him says.

"She is tonight."

"You know what I mean."

"Not really."

The male curses. "Yes, you do, Nar. What's gotten into you?"

"I won the first night, and we didn't shed a single tooth or claw. Be happy."

"I'm homicidal."

"That works too."

I remain quiet, thinking about where he's taking me because it's not to my hole. My hole is in the opposite direction. After a while, the males stop, and he puts me down and pats my head. "Good puppy. You did well." He nods as if

27

affirming calling me a puppy is just the thing I needed to hear.

We stand at a single large secluded tent at the edge of a sparsely treed forest. Beyond the forest is a clearing, a river, then a hill. I want to remove my makeshift hat so I can take in more of my surroundings, but can't because my hands are tied.

"Don't even think about it," the other male says to Nar, the one who bundled me up.

Nar's staring past the trees, a wishful look on his face.

"Stop looking at the border and get in," the other male adds and pushes past the tent's flap inside. Nar follows his friend, leaving me outside and instantly dread forms in my belly. He's going to leave me out here bound and unable to move. Shit. What have I done? I can only move an inch at a time so I inch toward the flap, trying to make my way inside.

"Nar, the female?" the other male says from the tent.

Clawed hands spring out of the tent, and I yelp as Nar grabs me and pulls me inside. He bends and starts untying my feet.

"I tied them too tightly," he says.

"Hence she cannot walk inside the tent," the other explains.

"Thank you, Mas. You can fuck off now. I'm good."

"Oh no." The male named Mas, the one with lighter hair, sits on a...a round wooden log, then props his elbows on his knees, eyes on me. "I'm intent on babysitting you."

Babysitting me or his friend? He's looking at me, and the way he licks his lips makes me glance away. Gur looks at me that way. As if he wants to eat me, and not in a sexy way, but in a real creepy way.

Once he loosened my feet, Nar rises and starts untying the top.

"This is Nar," Mas says, introducing us. "I'm Mas. Nar has gone crazy, and we're all gonna die."

"Don't be dramatic," Nar says as he releases the upper ties. I grab the pelt and tuck it around me, eyeing a firepit with logs in front of Mas's feet.

"You still cold?" Nar asks.

I nod.

From the moment that Gur and Feli touched me, I noticed their feverish skin. This alien species runs hot, hotter than humans. In more ways than just one. I'd never seen men built like this or spoken to males as forward and commanding as these. While I acknowledge their masculine appeal, I'm also uncomfortable with it. Thoughts about how attractive another alien species is are taboo on Earth. We don't have those thoughts, and I don't like that I'm having a hard time not watching Nar's upper body, especially the muscles that almost make his tattoos move over his skin as he fires up the pit at Mas's feet.

I approach almost immediately and stick my hands out, seeking warmth. I stare at the crackling fire while they both stare at me. I rub my hands as they thaw out. I'd love a shower and a cup of chicken soup, maybe a box of ice cream and an old romance movie. I'd love a week of that so I don't have to deal with my reality. But I want to live, and in order to live, I need to know who's my enemy and who's a friend. Are these two my friends?

I look up to see they're still staring.

"My name is Michelle," I say. "I come from Earth. It's illegal to treat me like a prisoner or to…to sell me to the highest bidder."

"You're a prize in our games," Mas says. "Neither of those things apply."

"Gur can't give me away. I'm not his to give away is what I mean. He will pay for this."

Nar moves to sit beside Mas. "How?" he asks.

"My brother will come for me."

"And then?"

"He'll take me back home. We have technology you don't have. If you keep me alive until he comes, he'll reward you."

Nar tilts his head. "I'll keep you alive."

Mas glares at Nar's profile. I don't know what they're planning. I don't know anything. I don't even know where I am. Nobody would tell me, not that I'd have understood since they provided me a translator just this morning. I haven't had a normal conversation in days, maybe weeks. I don't know. I just don't know.

Nar stands, and he's at me in a second. Startled by his rapid movement, I jump back, but he grabs me and envelops me in a hug. He picks me up and moves me to sit on his lap near the fire, his arms tight around me. "Don't fear anything."

I stare at his profile while he watches the other male.

Mas's jaw shifts left, then right. It's so crazy that I think I imagined it. I blink, waiting for him to do it again, but he rises with a groan. "I can't help you feed her, Nar. She can't accept anything from me unless she wants to warm my bed for the night."

Nar starts growling from deep in his chest, and I wiggle in his lap, trying to escape when I feel him grow hard. I freeze. Oh my God, he's hard, and he's so big, I can feel it through his kilt and the two pelts covering my ass. Swallowing, I bite my lip, not really wanting the other one to leave, mainly because I don't want to be alone with the one who's now stroking the fur on my back.

Mas continues, "The female is in distress, cold, and hungry. How will you feed her? We know they don't hunt."

"So there's no chicken soup?" I ask, knowing there never was. I'm dumb or desperate or both. *Sheltered little Michelle,* my brother would say to me, poking fun at how our late father spoiled me. As I was the youngest of three, my older siblings took the brunt of Daddy's anger. He never hurt me. But my siblings did. Sometimes emotionally, sometimes physically. and yet they kept sheltering me from the world. This was supposed to be my escape. Get to Joylius, check in with my brother, and disappear. I disappeared, all right.

"They eat our flesh, so I'm good," Nar says.

"They who?" There's more of us here?

Nar glances at me, but says nothing.

There *are* more of us. I think there are! I have to find them, join with them. Maybe they know how we can return. Or make it to Joylius, at least. But we don't eat their flesh. Hell no.

Mas leaves the tent, Nar's gaze following him, but shortly returning to me. He parts the pelt and strokes the collar around my neck, trailing a claw down the leather leash. He fists the leash and tugs, bringing me closer. Our faces inches apart, he whispers, "If you play the games with me and only me, I promise to hand you back to your brother when he comes. If you betray me, female, we both die."

"Gur told me not to accept your gift."

Nar nods. "Of course he did. I am a Ka. And you betrayed him. Why?"

"For the pelt." I say. "I was cold."

"Survival makes us think better, make smarter decisions."

Maybe. Maybe not. "I have no reason to trust you."

"You have no reason not to, whereas with Gur, you have every reason not to trust him. Am I right?"

I nod, knowing full well this male is going to take advantage of his night with me. He won't spare me his lust, and I need to mentally prepare for what's coming.

CHAPTER FIVE

NAR

Light on my lap, the female feels nice and cuddly. A puppy, really. I stroke the leash attached to her collar, imagining what she'd look like under me wearing only that. Behind my kilt, my cock is hard and ready to fuck, but I don't scent arousal from her, so I make no move to kiss her lips, which have turned a richer shade now.

It's the blood, I realize. This species is sensitive to cold. They run cold, so if it's colder outside than inside their bodies, their lips turn blue or purple. They're less agile than us too. I'm gonna enjoy keeping her warm and maybe take her for a run sometime. "Are you hungry?" I ask.

She blinks as if pulled out of a trance, and I release the leash.

"I would appreciate dry clothes. If you have any to spare."

"I'm disappointed you want to remain clothed."

Red colors her cheeks, and I touch them to feel the heat. Interesting. What's even more interesting is she's not asking about the medicine I showed her on my palm, the one Hart and I found in her pod when we stole it from Gur's camp not more than a few spans ago. I find it odd. Hart's female, the other womankind, seemed to believe this female needed the medicine. For now, I won't bring it up. I want to see if she asks. She's a quiet female, scared and confused and I know Gur hasn't treated her well.

"I am also hungry," she admits.

I dreaded this moment. It means I have to leave her to hunt or carve out my own piece of flesh so she can roast it over the fire. For a brutal alien race who eats the flesh of predators, their females are awfully cute. Kind of like a peatania, a cute furry little animal with a venomous bite that causes paralysis. I'd know. I've been bitten three times, and once with Mas. It left us lying on the forest floor like two logs while bugs bit and annoyed us for three spans. I couldn't scratch any bites, and my hunter waged a war under my skin, unable to crawl out because venom caused temporary neural paralysis. Good times.

Thinking about Mas makes me wonder where he went. He's not happy with me, and to be honest, I'm not thrilled with myself either. Though I forgive myself for forgetting about killing Gur and what Hart sent me to do, and taking the female instead. She smells divine. Like a fertile womb, youth, and family, something I never even thought I wanted. But I smelled her underpants, and I started wanting. There's no going back, especially not now that I have the real thing in my lap.

Her lips, this close to mine, make me want to lean in and kiss her, and I do lean in, and when she doesn't lean back, I tilt my head and connect our lips. Hers feel cold to me, and a shiver runs down my spine. I sniff and scent no arousal, but I also scent no fear, so that's a win for me. My brother's human female reeked of fear the times that I came near her. In conclusion, I'm better with females than he is.

"I brought you clothes," I whisper again in that same soft love-bug voice. I am so proud of that new voice I found for her that I feel like patting myself on the back. She'll be begging for my hook soon.

"Can I have them?"

"Kiss me, and I'll give them to you."

She smiles. "You're a piece of work."

"Carved from a hooker father and a mother I can't remember, I'm an art piece around here."

She chuckles.

It's a nice sound and lifts her eyes at the corners. I smile back. She takes one look at my smile, and hers is gone. She stares at my mouth while I hear her heartbeat accelerate, fear lacing her pleasant scent.

"What just happened?" I ask. "Why are you afraid?"

"I am not."

"I smell prey's fear."

She swallows and looks away, but I can't let her. I move her chin so she'll face me again. "What is it?"

Her gaze drops to my mouth, and I can't tell if she wants to kiss me or not.

"You have a fierce smile," she says.

"And?"

"It's scary."

"Awww, puppy, you'll get used to it."

She chuckles again, then picks a leather string on her pelt, eyeing me warily, pink coloring her cheeks again. I stroke the place where I see the most color. I have no idea why this is happening, but she leans into my touch, then lifts a fragile hand and strokes my jaw with clawless fingers. Her face moves closer and closer, and she closes her eyes, pecks my lips, then pulls back.

I don't think so. I fist the leash and force her to stay close. I keep kissing her, coaxing her mouth to open so I can taste her while suppressing the instinct to devour her whole. When I taste the sweetness of her tongue, I moan and grab the back of her head, tilting it for better access and kiss her. A rumbling sound I don't recognize rises out of my chest, and I'm so shocked at the tone that I separate from her lips and stare at her dumbfounded.

"You purr," she says, looking as dumbfounded as I am.

Why yes, I do, although I haven't ever made this particular sound before. I do it again, this time deliberately, and watch that blush color her cheeks.

"What's it mean?" I ask.

She clears her throat. "What's what mean?"

I point. "The coloring of cheeks. The blush comes and goes."

Looking away, she plays with strings. "I want my clothes."

"Answer me."

"That wasn't what we agreed on. I kiss you and get clothes."

To press her about the blushing or not to press her? I decide not to press, but to honor my end of the deal. "They're in the sack on the other end." I point to the partition in the tent which we throw sacks behind. "Over there."

She slides off my lap, and while I watch her walk away, I adjust my erection and extend my hearing outward, listening for Mas. He's not around. Where has he gone? While in enemy territory, we shouldn't separate. Even with the truce between my tribe and the Ra, they're still the enemy. Our peace lasts as long as it takes for me to snatch and secure small prey. It'll be a short time when war breaks out again.

It bothers me that Mas is alone out there, not because I think he can't take care of himself, but because I'm not with him, and if anything should happen to him, I would take revenge and slaughter half this camp before they had a chance to kill me. Hart would then avenge my death, and so on and so forth, and for turns and turns, we'd war, until the Ka or the Ra or both were exterminated.

The female, whose name I can only pronounce in my head, walks into the separate part of the tent, and I hear her rummaging through the sacks, dressing. She walks out wearing blue pants and a yellow shirt cut off at the shoulders. The clothes seem too big for her small frame, and I wonder why this species dresses in such a...an ugly way. The females ought to wear tight-fitting corsets the way our goddesses might, to show us their feminine curves and beauty so that we can worship them.

The female returns to sit by the fire and crosses one leg over the other, gaze on her foot. The five small toes, instead of our four, are painted pink, the same color as the blush on her cheeks. I conclude she likes to coordinate colors.

"Do you happen to have shoes?" she asks.

I stretch out my legs, turn my foot, examine my boot against her bare foot. Mine won't fit her, but maybe I can snatch one off a smaller male. Nah, there's no males with feet that small. Our feet are also wider to allow for better balance and to absorb the impact on the spine when we land from great heights.

"You won't be doing any walking," I announce, and secure the pelt she shrugged off back around her. I glare at her bare feet. Their bareness is bothering me. I haven't thought this through, and fucking Gur kept this cold-sensitive creature with no shoes. She could've frozen and died. What is wrong with that motherfucker? A snarl builds in my chest, but I suppress it so I don't scare her more than I already have.

I crouch in front of her so I can bundle her up again.

"What are you doing?"

"Gonna take you hunting."

"I don't hunt."

"Not for food, pup, for shoes." A worn-out leather string breaks, and I snarl. Motherfucker. I knew this string would break sooner or later, and I never replaced it, always having more pressing issues than a string on my pelt.

"Can't I buy shoes anywhere?" she asks.

I nod, familiar with selling and trade. We melt metal and make coins from it, though the Ka haven't used coins for anything because we need nothing we can't provide for ourselves. "We can, but..." I lean back, scrubbing my jaw when I sense Mas at the entrance. Immediately, my hunter rises, irritated that a male stepped into the place where I'm with a female. A growl builds in my chest, and I cough so Mas doesn't recognize it for what it is: a threat that I wanna tear and kill.

"You're gonna choke on your own blood if you keep growling at me, Nar."

Mas brought back a skinned and prepped prey. He offers it to me, and I stand and shake my head, noting his other hand is folded behind his back. He's hiding something. If it were anyone else, I'd make them show me both hands.

"Don't be stubborn," he says. "You can accept it if she can't."

"We were just going hunting," I tell him.

Mas glances at the female, then back at me, a smile playing on his lips, a chuckle reverberating in his chest. I roll my eyes just before he throws back his head and laughs.

"Hahaha," I mock him, although, we both know womankind don't hunt. They walk around the hunting grounds collecting flowers and marking territories they shouldn't be marking. I can't hunt and leave her here. I have to accept his catch. I snatch the koiama from his hand, and just when I think he's done for the span, he lifts the hand behind his back and shows me a bunch of long prepped sticks. That's for the female. Womankind use weapons to cut predator flesh into pieces, line up the cubes on sticks, and heat them up a little before consumption. It is all very disturbing to me, but it is what it is.

I snatch the sticks from him too.

He smirks and reaches behind him again and pulls out a boyus flower to sniff the pleasant aroma it emits.

"That's for me, right?" I ask, irritated as fuck.

"Right." He offers me the flower, and I think my male hunter just died inside me as I accept a flower from another male.

"Awww," the female says.

I think we're done here. "Get out, Mas."

He winks and leaves. I stand there as the weight of his departure settles on my chest. "Don't go too far," I call out.

"Mmhm."

"I mean it."

"I heard you."

He heard me, but that doesn't mean he'll listen. Gur needs to die, and Mas can tell I won't be the one executing him. Mission failed. But hey, the female looks excited at the prospect of food and dick. All will be well.

CHAPTER SIX

MICHELLE

Before sitting on the stool, the male takes out a dagger. I scoot away, his dagger making me nervous. I've never seen such a barbaric species, and culture shock is a real thing. On Joylius, the only other place where I've met native alien species, even before humans colonized it, the natives weren't this primitive or even humanoid. His near-human appearance normalizes him, and it's almost as if he was made to appear less threatening than he really is. There's an edge to him I can't quite identify.

He tilts his head. "What's the matter again?"

"I've never seen a dead animal before," I lie. *I've never seen anyone like you.*

"You'll get used to that too."

He sounds irritated, so I sit by the warm fire, extending my feet toward it, keeping them warm while my mind wanders back to the adjacent small space and the sacks full of fur I found there. I wonder if I can have an extra one to cover my feet.

"After I feed you, we're going hunting," he says as he starts carving the animal's flesh. My belly churns. I stand, intent on getting another fur, but trip and twist, trying not to land on my face. I thump on my side instead. Heat crawls over my cheeks, and I look behind me to where the male sits, unmoving, eyes wider than before.

"I was on my way to get more fur, if that's okay with you." Sitting up on the floor, I struggle to move my arm and push the hair out of my eyes. He tied the pelt across my arms and knees, and I feel like a potato sack again. I blow on my hair, but it's wet and sticking to my face. "Can't a girl get a break here?" I push against the pelt, kicking, wriggling, trying to get out of it and unable to. Frustrated, I thrash on the floor, practically growling, mad I can't help myself with anything in this place.

I bite the pelt and growl, rejoicing when I catch a string between my teeth. I tug it by moving my head, untie it, release my arms enough to free them, and pull off the pelt. I get up and move my hair out of my face, then rip the leather string off the pelt and use it to secure my hair behind my head. "There." I step out of the pelt that's trapping my legs and look up.

Nar's caught midmovement, leaning forward as if to rise, but then freezing in place, watching me, eyes like saucers.

I huff and walk away.

From the variety of furs in the sacks, I pull out a beautiful one with soft, long brown hairs. I bring it to my face and stroke my cheek with it as I return to lay it beside the fire so I can sit on the floor and across from Nar.

"What kind of animal is this?" I ask, crossing my legs.

"It's not an animal." He's cutting up the food.

"What do you mean?"

"It's a male. A Ra long-hair."

I frown, not understanding, but he puts a stick piled with meat that he cut up over the fire. The sizzling reminds me how hungry I am. Gur threw raw meat at me down in the hole a few times, but I wouldn't eat it, so they fed me herbs and even flowers, though not the same kind of flower Mas brought.

Nar offers me a stick with seared meat on it, and finally, I'm warm and I'm going to eat, maybe even drink clean water. If I could shower, I'd be set.

I accept with a thank-you and tear into it as if I hadn't eaten in days or weeks, so fast, I nearly choke on the deliciously tender meat. "This is really good," I say with my mouth full, my ladylike behavior all but history.

"I'm a good hunter," comes from outside the tent.

Nar grinds his sharp teeth. Those teeth are scary, and he's easier to look at with his mouth closed. Still, he's funny when annoyed, and I chuckle.

He bares his teeth and growls, then bites down on the dead uncooked animal, crushing the bone along with the meat. I gape as he chews and swallows in seconds. A small bone appears between his lips, and he takes it with his thumb and a forefinger and proceeds to clean his teeth with it. He spits on the floor and flicks the bone off to one side.

I stare, barely able to close my gaping mouth.

"What?" he barks.

Oh, a million and one things. First, his jaws are so powerful, they crushed the animal's bones, and he swallowed without having to chew much. I don't say that, but offer this instead: "The table at my brother's house is set daily at the same time in three-hour increments during the day starting at eight in the morning. We dine at a table set with plates, glasses, and utensils, which we use for eating."

He nods. "You're sitting, using a stick now. If you can stop staring at me for a moment"—he winks—"you've got all you need."

I chuckle. "I was just trying to explain why I'm staring at

you. It's all so different from what I'm used to on Earth." Or Mars. Or Joylius, for that matter.

"You're welcome to assess my fitness, female."

I chew my food, trying not to keep staring at the broad shoulders or abs or the muscular thighs his kilt reveals when parted.

"A female living with her brother is unmated," he says.

I am "unmated." Thirty-two and unmated. I've refused all the suitors my brother chose for me, thereby not securing an alliance with a powerful family. Meanwhile, eager to marry, my older sister took it upon herself to secure an alliance for us. Trouble is, the man she wants set his sights on me. Hence, I left for an extended vacation to Joylius from which I never intended to return. Among other reasons, I needed the general of National Security to forget me and give my sister his full attention.

"You seem...sad," Nar says.

Sighing, I twirl my stick. "Most women my age are already married, and I'm used to having to deflect people's questions when they bring up marriage."

"Does that make you sad? That you're not mated?"

I shrug. "Sometimes, but I have reasons."

"Not to worry. You will mate as soon as you finish your kebab."

"Oh no, that's not what I meant."

"You've assessed my fitness."

Jesus! "I wasn't assessing your...fitness." I *was* assessing his fitness, and I can't believe he called me out on it. Gentlemen don't do that. I'm way out of my comfort zone here on the floor in a tent in the midst of an alien race that looks like they can't decide if they want to eat me or breed me. Maybe both.

"What are you doing when you're looking at me?" he prods.

I flush and pick at my stick. "I'm just looking."

"Are you shy?"

"Maybe you're too blunt. Ever thought about that?" What the hell. "I don't want to talk anymore."

He leans in. "That works for me."

Shit, I walked into that one. I place the last piece of meat aside and lie down, covering my head with the fur.

The male laughs, and I hear him chewing, moving around, then nothing. I peer over the pelt. The tent stands empty. The fire crackles, and I see he placed more wood at the top. Maybe he won't return for a while. Where has he gone? Wait a second. I'm alone and outside instead of inside the hole I can't crawl out of to escape. Is this my chance?

I throw off the pelt and leap up, tiptoe to the tent flap, and poke my head out. It's still raining, and there're muddy puddles everywhere. I have no shoes, don't know where I am, and my pod carrying the clothes I carried onboard could've crashed anywhere.

Nar appears before me, and I gasp and pull my head back. I remain standing in place and staring at the flap.

He pokes his head inside and smiles, pale eyes lifting at the corners. "Did you miss me?"

"I wanted some fresh air."

"Mmhm. Get some rest. We're gonna be up all night." He wags his eyebrows.

"No."

He snorts. "I won a night with the prize. The prize submits to the winner."

I shake my head.

He nods his, and it makes me want to slap the arrogance off his face. Frustrated, I turn and get back under the pelt. No way am I sleeping with an alien. It's taboo and wrong, and if my brother heard of it, he'd disown me. A disowned woman in my society never gets to Mars, and Mars is our future. Earth is just a place for the labor force dictated to by the corporate monopolies living on Mars. One of many reasons why people are fleeing Earth.

CHAPTER SEVEN

NAR

When we wage wars, we wage them with weapons and on two feet. A hunter hunts, gathers, and is less capable of the strategic thinking necessary to win battles than a male. In hunter, our basic instinct is the killer instinct. Oftentimes on a battlefield, it's the last resort, a survival instinct. In a losing battle, the hunter often retreats. A self-preservation instinct. Therefore, catching a hunter on the retreat while I'm on two legs and then slaying said hunter is incredibly hard.

A pelt of hunter's fur is the ultimate war trophy, one I'm sure Gur would love to attain. He's never caught one of the Ka males and hates that I showed up for his games dressed in his male's fur. Not to mention, wrapping my female in it gives me perverse pleasure. I'm gonna fuck her on the fur of one of Gur's males.

Mas gives me a side-eye, then wiggles his nose and taps it.

He smells my arousal. "I'm thinking about the female," I say.

He stands up and moves away from the tent, turning up his face, letting the rain soak his body. Goddess, I hate the weather in this part of Ra territory with a passion of the thousand pelts I've made of their dead males.

Mas spreads his arms. "They will bathe like this in our blood, Nar."

"Come here, Drama Boy." I tap the log he sat on. "Sit with me, and let's have a think."

"The rain washed away the last shred of Nar, and I am left with a horny love bug buzzing around the female. The goddess won't show me the way, not with you determined to claim the female instead of doing what we came here to do. Why, oh, why did Hart send me with you? Is it to torture me? Have I sinned?"

I roll my eyes far back, and my head follows. "Sit down, Mas."

"Your arousal makes me itchy."

I know what he means. Back home, the scent of my brother's arousal when around his female or even when not around her made me itchy too. It's a scent we've only recently encountered and aren't used to. Arousal from killing prey or slaying a male smells different. There's also anger and hunger and other scents mixed with it, so it's never alone. I understand what Mas means, though I hope the scent becomes something common for my people, something we encounter so often, we can ignore it. "I'm not hard anymore." I tap his log.

He walks back and moves the log a few steps away from me. "Liar." He sits down and gives me his annoyed face.

I scrub my beard. Gonna cut it, maybe braid it like Mas does his. His beard is neat, and I don't want my female looking at him all neat. "Can you craft me some of those beads?" I point at his beard.

He walks up and knocks on my head. "It's all wind inside," he says, meaning my head is empty and winds blow through from one ear to the other. I bat his hand away, and he sits back down with a chuckle. I can't tell him I wanna go hunting because the female needs shoes. I think if I do, he might leave me out here, which would be to leave me for dead. We both know Gur rigged the games so neither of us can win, or if we happen to win, we'll need an exit plan, which was precisely why Mas planned not to win, only to compete against Gur, who should've entered the games. "We're fucked."

"Finally, you come around," Mas says. "Yes, please, do continue."

"We are super fucked. Fuckety fucked."

He's nodding, leaning in, waiting for me to come up with something, to help us proceed forward because we need a plan for tomorrow and we need to set something up today, maybe even tonight when the Ra are sleeping, when only the guards roam the camp. But the female needs shoes, and all I can think about is how I'm gonna get her shoes. I can't make them or produce them out of thin air. We stole her pod, and Hart gave all her clothes to his female, leaving this one with very little.

Though it didn't escape my notice how the clothes I brought from the pod seemed too large for Michelle's frame, as if they didn't belong to her. Since her people's fashion isn't familiar to me I don't really know how they wear clothes, only that they cover the parts they waste from, which is terribly inefficient. Our vertos are a better choice. She ought to have worn the one dress I brought.

"Anything else?" Mas asks, anticipating something from me.

"I got nothing."

"You have the wind."

I chuckle because an irritated Mas is funny.

"Don't laugh," he says, serious, and I laugh again, then see

Mas's hunter pushing to the surface, flashing me with his eyes, drawing out mine.

My heartbeats accelerate, muscles relax, bones begin rearranging, and I growl. "I'll sleep on it," I say.

"We can't sleep on it."

"We have to."

"Gur is out there"—Mas points in the direction of the platform—"planning on killing you when you win and—"

"You think I'll win?"

Mas curses and walks away.

"Hey!" I shout after him.

He parts his verto and shows me his bare ass.

I laugh. "I'm gonna have something for you soon."

"I doubt it," he throws over his shoulder.

"Where are you going?"

"Elsewhere."

"Come back and sleep here tonight." He lost the dry shelter the tent provides, and now I truly feel bad. "I mean that."

"I heard you." Mas disappears from sight, and I stay out here, listening to the rain, watching it hit the puddles, wondering where I'm gonna get her shoes. The shoes win the female. Tomorrow, when she gets up onto that platform and has to spend the entire span there, rain or shine, she'll wish she could move over the wet, dirty, cold floor, and I can tell this female isn't used to discomfort. It's in the fine way she eats, taking little bites, chewing thoroughly before swallowing, making sure her blunt teeth don't make a mess. It's refined and...and feminine. Like a goddess.

A thought occurs to me. If Amti lives among us and with Hart, what if another goddess decided to take up the flesh of womankind. Bera? Mae? Or maybe even Herea, goddess of the hunt? No, no, neither of those. I rack my brain, trying to think if I had unknowingly called up a goddess, but can't think of anything like what happened with my brother Hart, who called up Amti, goddess of madness and lust, then pissed on a fire, effectively marking the goddess for himself.

Thunder and lightning strikes in the distance, lighting up the camp.

I walk back inside and see the female bundled under the pelt. Smiling, I get cozy on her fur-made bed.

CHAPTER EIGHT

MICHELLE

T he alien lies down, his body not touching mine, so I'm trying not to freak about the fact he's behind me while I lie on my side. I fist the corner of the pelt he gave me the way a toddler might fist her comfort object. The fire's dying down. The temperature has dropped, and minutes later, I can't feel my toes. A shiver runs down arms, and I'm cold again with partially wet hair.

"I know you're awake," he says in a voice laced with something terribly sexy. A soft rumble emanates from his chest. I think he's purring. I'm fond of cats, always have been, have three at home I'm unlikely to ever see again. At least I know my sister will care for them.

Not that the male is a cat, far from it, but he's sort of a lion. He even has a thick dark brown mane of hair that he tames by braiding. I don't answer him, figuring if I don't speak, he'll fall asleep and forget about the night he's owed. I don't owe him anything. I do not. Even though he likely saved me from hypothermia, has fed me, clothed me, provided me with a better shelter than the hole in the ground, I still owe him nothing, and least of all sex.

Minutes pass, and I wish I had a watch or a clock on the wall. How do they tell time? By the sun or moon, most likely, something I can't do. It's definitely late afternoon, and approaching night. The camp has gone quiet. Is he not going to stack the fire for the night? I'm cold and don't dare move for fear I'll have to face him.

Behind me, he lifts the pelt covering me and moves closer. I can't see him, but I hear the purr, and oh, is that heat at my back? I think it is. I think his body radiates heat, and when it's quiet like this, all I can do is focus on the warmth, the necessity of it for sustaining my life right now.

Nevertheless, I stay in my place.

He does too, but continues purring. I listen to the sound, which somehow settles my nerves. My eyelids droop, and I close them. If I fall asleep and freeze, I'll never wake up. I snap open my eyes. God, why does my brain have to think all the time?

My back feels warm, while my extremities are practically numb. I tuck my arms between my legs, trying to get them warmed up, then curl into a ball.

The male chuckles. "Every species in the universe has a basic survival instinct. Even prey, mostly prey, actually, because how else will they survive when faced with a preda-tor? Fighting the instinct generally leads to death. Following the instinct leads to survival and winning." He pauses, maybe waiting for me to respond. I won't.

"Your body knows it needs heat," he continues. "I have what you want, and yet you're refusing the instinct, and while you're resisting, you're also freezing. When I am faced with hard choices, I ask myself one question."

A long pause stretches, and I'm all ears, but he's not saying anything. What is it? I pinch my lips together, forcing myself not to ask.

"It's a simple question, and when answered, I have more

clarity of thought and can act on thoughts that produce results. I don't like to sit around and wait for others to make decisions for me."

What's he saying? He'll make decisions for me if I don't decide on what to do about my current situation?

"Because," he says at my ear, and my heart speeds up as he moves my hair away from my neck, then touches his lips to my skin, "when you give other people the power to make decisions for you, you've transferred the power to them. So ask me where we are right now."

I say nothing.

A claw traces from the corner of my eye to my neck, and he purrs louder.

"I've made a decision for you." He grabs my hip and pulls me closer to him, trapping my cold feet between his. He covers my two hands with his one. "The thing I regret is starting the fire in the first place. There will be no fire tonight or tomorrow. The only heat you get is from my body. I am certain you will make a choice now that you see I will take action anyway."

"So you'll do what you want, but it's going to be on my terms or yours. Is that what you're saying?"

"When you accepted my gift, I won a night and the right to mount you."

"I don't want you to mount me."

"Nevertheless, you took the pelt, the fire, the shelter, the food, and you are a prize in our games."

Tears accumulate in my eyes. I'm helpless. Sure, I can snarl and snap at him, get pissed off and start running around or running away, though I'm fairly certain the smartest thing to do is to stay with this alien. I have nowhere to run, and night on this planet is brutal. I'd know. I spent the first night after crashing alone, and I nearly froze to death. In the morning, Feli found me shivering and tossed me a fur coat. If he hadn't, I'd have frozen the next night. But I won't completely fold under his pressure either.

I turn and look up at him. He stares me down with white eyes, and I think if I make a move, I get to set the pace. If I do nothing, he'll set the pace for the night. Even though I have no illusions he's manipulating me into doing what he wants, I scoot closer and peck his lips, then lean back to see a bright color show up behind the white of his eyes. He leans in slowly as if not to scare me off and returns the kiss.

"My people," he says at my lips, "kiss a lot. Or they used to when we had females."

He props his palm on the floor and rises up over me, effectively caging me in while he keeps kissing my mouth, coaxing me to open mine. His purr is steady, soft, seductive, and I run a palm down his biceps. He feels like strength and power. No swimmer, no bodybuilder, no athlete is built quite this strong or has this array of different-sized muscles so clearly defined. Since his palm is on the floor, when he bends at the elbow, it reminds me of push-ups, except he doesn't push up. Instead, he kisses me again, this time also tilting his head and swiping his tongue over my lips.

"Open," he growls.

He holds his entire weight on one arm, and I move my hand over his biceps, feeling peaks and valleys of muscle. It awakens something...hungry inside me. The men I've seen walking in and out of our house, the suitors my brother chose, all wore suits, ties, or, at the very least, tailored jackets. They were clean-shaven, smelling of various colognes, and the only jewelry they wore were expensive bulky watches.

This male is raw and wears more jewelry in his hair than I do.

Slowly, I move my palm from his arm to his chest, where I feel the tendons and muscles that strain as he holds his position without dropping his weight on me.

"You are admiring my fitness," he concludes with a sniff, wiggling his nose in that inhuman way.

He pushes up and spreads my legs.

I gasp and close them.

Snarling, he parts them again and kneels between them. "Resist your instincts to fuck me, and I will tie you up. Maybe I will tie you up anyway."

I shake my head.

"No what? You won't resist your instinct, or you don't want to be tied up?"

I swallow. "Both." Neither. I don't know. My heart beats wildly.

Sitting back on his heels, eyes locked with mine, he does nothing further, and I can't maintain eye contact, though I want to. His torso is unscarred, fuzzy with tiny hairs I barely see. There's an eight-pack with corded muscle on the sides.

"Do you want to see the rest of my fitness?" He removes his belt and stretches out his hand, making a show of dropping it on the floor. His kilt, he unsnaps and lets fall down his hips, revealing his penis. He's long, too long, too wide, too big, and there's something at the tip. The penis twitches, and clear fluid spurts out of the tip to slide down the mushroom top and the length of him.

I lick my lips, then snap my eyes up, my face burning. It's getting hot in here. He did say he'd keep me warm, and he's pretty great at it.

He grabs my leash and winds it about his fist. I'd forgotten about that. It's been my constant companion since I arrived here. He tugs, and I sit up. He pulls me closer so our faces are inches apart.

"I despise your fashions," he says and presses his cheek to mine, rubbing like a cat might. He smells…masculine. Heavy. Spicy. Strong. My nipples perk and my breasts feel heaver as his warm front touches them when he leans in and reaches behind me. He grunts, and I hear a tear. A brush of cold air between my legs tells me he tore the jeans. There's a hole between my legs.

"I'd have undressed," I say.

"You'll still undress," he whispers at my ear, then moves my hair behind my ear and kisses under the ear where I'm most sensitive. Butterflies flutter in my belly, and I close my eyes, enjoying the way he moves his mouth over the side of my neck.

A claw rips right down the middle of the shirt, and he parts it, then touches my right breast. My breasts are small, and his big hand cups one, rolling the nipple. I suppress a moan while my belly grows heavy with...with arousal.

It is wrong. It is wrong, wrong, wrong.

I should not be aroused, for many reasons, the biggest one being that this is a male of a different species applying coercion, using my helpless state for his gain. I shouldn't like how he kisses me, how he purrs steadily from his chest, making my head fuzzy with wild thoughts of this male fucking me into the ground, pressing me, forcing his way inside me and me liking it all, begging him for more.

He moves back up and kisses my mouth again, and this time I open and receive his tongue. He groans, and I close my eyes because his purr reverberates in my head like a tune I want to sway to.

A hand fists my hair.

I press my palms over his chest, and under them, his muscles move. We kiss with passion, turning our heads, breathing heavily, and I slide my palms down his torso when he thrusts up, effectively positioning his cock between my hands. He tugs my hair back and forces me to look up so I don't see what he's doing while looking at me with strange orange behind the white of his eyes. He swipes a finger over his lips, leaving them glistening. Bending, he pecks my mouth, and I taste something sweet and spicy, yet potent and bold, and I think this is his semen. I lick my lips, wanting to taste more.

He moves me farther away and sucks my bottom lip, then slowly, gripping my hair, moves my body to bend toward his middle. His cock is pulsing, pushing out liquid with each pulse. Using his thumb, he picks up some and smears it over my mouth. I taste again, moaning out loud this time. His seed makes my mouth water, my entire body buzzes, and I'm overheated now, almost feverish.

He smirks and tugs the collar, gently guiding me where he wants me. I scoot back as I put him in my mouth and suck. His hand in my hair hurts as he clutches it, sometimes tugging up as I move down and over his length with my mouth. The semen dribbles on my tongue, and I keep swallowing, thinking this is the best thing I've tasted on this planet. I hold him with two hands and stroke, milking him, loving how this part of him is rock hard and responsive, spurting seed in my mouth. When I grab his balls and squeeze, the male freezes, and a burst of seed gushes into my mouth, spilling out the sides. He places his one hand over two of mine holding them in place, not letting me stroke.

He jerks my leash, and I sit up, feeling seed running down my chin.

His eyes are a blaze of orange, with tiny vertically slit pupils.

I wipe my mouth, a little apprehensive that he practically stopped me from blowing him all the way. Actually, I'm quite embarrassed, unsure what happens next.

But he's sure. I barely understand him when he says in a strangled voice, "Good night." He dresses and leaves the tent.

CHAPTER NINE

NAR

Drunk on the pleasure she gave me, I didn't notice that my hunter had risen to the surface until hunger for the female breached my rational brain. I felt the hunter and his strange behavior while I was trying to enjoy the female. He makes me want to either eat her delicate flesh or fuck her, or maybe I want both. In the moment, the two instincts, both primal in nature, are conflicted, and I stepped outside to clear my head.

The hunter eats prey.

The male fucks females.

That's how it's always been with my people, or at least that's what I've seen older males do with females when I was younger. Males and females have sex. Hunters hunt. We don't mix the two, so when my hunter rose up and practically roared in my head, bidding the female a good night seemed appropriate. I would regret eating her. I'd rather breed her.

"Mas," I hiss into the night, hoping he's not too far to hear me. When he doesn't answer, I walk around the tent to check if he's sleeping and just too lazy to get up. Circling back to the tent's flap, I call out again.

"Shut up, Ka!" multiple Ra males shout from the tents in the camp closest to us.

I roll my eyes and call out again, a little louder now.

The Ra stir, and I hear them rising from beds, padding across the ground, some in hunter, which only makes my hunter more aggressive. Growly Ra hunters poke their heads out of the tents, showing me their teeth, their silver eyes tiny dots in the night.

I pick up on a sprinting hunter coming right at me. Crouching, I bare my teeth and reach for my dagger. "Come at me, boy," I whisper, smiling, excited one of the Ra wants to steal my female from me. That's grounds for skinning him. My heart beats eagerly as I push back the hunter instinct. I love challenging death, and fighting another hunter while on two feet is definitely challenging death. A hunter is a beast. A male is just a male.

A light-brown, sun-kissed hunter comes around one tent, orange eyes glowing.

Mas.

Disappointed, I groan. Why isn't anyone trying to steal my female? Why can't they at least try?

"Fucking pussies," I shout.

Mas loops around another tent and slips in the mud, his hunter legs dancing as he tries to prevent a fall. Laughter rings out in the camp. I snort, suppressing my own laughter as Mas finds his balance and now prowls slowly toward me.

"The Ka hookholes aren't used to rough terrain," comes from one of the tents. "Go home, spring children."

I ignore the jabs and pat Mas's hunter on the head. He's covered in mud. Before entering the clean tent, he moves to the side to the water barrel we set up to collect rain for showering so we don't have to walk all the way to the river at the border to clean up. I follow him and open a small valve for the water to pour over him. Once he's clean, I smell blood and bend to take a better look.

Mas cut his flank. I swipe a finger over the wound and bring the finger to my nose, then sniff. Gravel. "What were you doing crossing the River Stones?"

The River Stones is the only dry place with this type of fine gravel. Spans ago, my brother and I crossed it when we snuck into the camp in search of the female. We left in a pod that's attached to one of our towers now.

I stand, hands on my hips, knowing Mas stays in hunter to heal the wounds. He's shaking now, both from cold and injury. I bet he slipped in the mud on purpose to cover up the wound so the Ka won't smell it. "Come in."

Mas tilts his head.

I walk to the tent and hear him following me. Even with a female inside, I can't leave Mas out here injured and cold. It's just not gonna happen, even though I hate having him near her. Once inside, I find her under the covers, back to the entrance. But that's not what catches my attention. Fire rages inside the pit. Fire I had put out. There's nothing in the tent that could've started the fire and nothing for her to use to start one. It makes me uncomfortable. Is there a goddess in the tent? Spirits? The hair stands on end at the back of my neck.

Mas settles in the corner near the entrance opposite her, whining as he starts licking his wound. I'm okay with Mas's hunter inside the tent with my female. I am. Really. Grinding my teeth, I sit on the fur before her, propping my arms on my knees, eyes on Mas. His hunter lifts his head, sees me guarding the female, and promptly turns around and gives me his big ass to look at. He snorts (because he's laughing at me) and buries his nose in the corner of the tent.

Mas all settled in hunter, I feel more confident that he

won't try to move in on her. I stare at the fire that's raging higher and higher. There's no wood for it to burn in this way. A million thoughts of why the fire rages with no wood go through my head. Talem oil. Meali oil. Gorischrome stone deposits. But only one idea sticks, because none of those things are in the tent or ever were in the tent.

A goddess came and lit the fire for my female. Or the female goddess set the fire for herself.

I scrub my jaw, uncomfortable with this line of thinking. Goddesses walking among us make me uneasy. Knowing they've returned to walk the lands and enslave the males into their service, their power, their bodies, makes me positively crazy. Mae is a goddess of fire and lies. As I sit by the raging fire, I listen to the thunder and hear rain starting up again.

Mae is said to have been born of fire on a night when snow covered the lands. The villagers gathered around to witness her birth, not knowing who she was. Frail and thin, with long black hair and pitch-black eyes, she lured all the females into the fire, leaving only the males, who served her till the end of their time. She had many males, but never stayed with one, until one seeded her with a boy with orange eyes. She named him Ka, and when he grew older, she took him as a lover too. The legend says they had a baby girl together, almost a replica of Mae, but crueler. Her name was Aoa.

Aoa tried to seduce her father, and when he refused, she directed a firelight bolt into his heart and burned him alive, then went on burning the males in the village. She claimed the territory for her own. Mae, grieved and disappointed in Aoa, left the village. Aoa claimed her victory the following morning, naming the new tribe after her father, Ka.

I slip outside and grab a bucket attached to the water tank. Back in the tent, I empty it over the fire. Mas stirs, and I feel him watching, but don't care about him witnessing my moment of madness. I worship Aoa, for she is the protector of my tribe, but I will not be a servant to her, in this life or the next. If I am to breed Aoa in her new flesh, she will be marked and belong only to me until the end of our time, not the end of my time.

Fire put out, I crawl under the covers with the female. I know she's awake and deliberately won't acknowledge my proximity. That's fine. I envelop her body with mine, noting her temperature. Like Mae and her daughter Aoa, she could have a frozen heart.

CHAPTER TEN

MICHELLE

The parted tent flap allows both light and wind inside. During the night, Nar put out the fire along with my hope this is some sort of bad dream I'm gonna awaken from and find my brother's face hovering over me, looking worried sick why I stayed in a dream-induced coma for so long. I chuckle. My brother would worry, all right. I'm his ticket to Mars.

While National Security reigns over Earth, it's Mars where the glamour and society had moved to. Those of us left on Earth are regarded as a different class, a secondary class, and my brother hates the notion that he's anything besides primary. If someone could get him to Mars, he'd trade his position in National Security. He'd also trade secrets, and has traded them for months, while I sat on pins and needles wondering when any of the gentlemen he met up with in secret would betray him and destroy us all in the process.

A burst of wind whistles through the tent, and I shudder under the covers. I don't want to leave the warm fur and face the day on the platform, where Gur's gonna parade me around like an animal to be acquired. Nar will do whatever it takes to win me, but what if it's not enough? What if I end up with someone who hurts me or worse?

Sucking Nar's dick didn't bother me as much as it should have. Touching his body definitely didn't bother me at all. And there's the taste of his semen. It's sweet and spicy, pleasant tasting, and as I recall the flavor, my mouth waters. Oh God, I'm gross. My thoughts are gross. Who is this person inside me? I don't recognize myself anymore. I'm not a lusty confused idiot. I'm Michelle, and I want to get up, get dressed, and face the day.

"Okay." I nod to reassure myself. Standing, I secure the large pelt around my body and rub my eyes as I walk outside. In the distance, toward the main camp, males march in military formation, their boots sloshing though mud. I pass the tent and hear chuckling. I tiptoe to the back of the tent and peek around it. Nar and his friend, Mas, stand before a large tanklike object, out of which water pours from two holes. They're nude, facing each other and chatting as if it's perfectly normal for two men to yap about bullshit while nude and hard and showering.

Nar's body entraps my gaze. He's got dips on the side of his ass, and he's so toned that the cords that make up his muscles are clearly outlined on his thigh. Because I'm staring, I don't notice when they quiet down.

They've seen me. There's no point in hiding, so I step out, clearing my throat. "I would love to shower," I say, then realize I forgot to add the *when you're done* part. What in God's name is happening to me? It's like Nar's body makes me stupid.

Nar extends a hand and flicks two fingers. "Join me."

I had that coming, didn't I? "I'll wait until you're done."

Mas snickers. "If you wait until he's done, he'll stand here for the span and waste all the water on purpose. You'd better catch some while you can."

To hold the pelt in place, I tuck the corner of it between my breasts, and I walk over.

"Mas," Nar says.

"Nar?" Mas smirks.

"Fuck off."

Mas scrubs his face and steps out from under his water spray, then points a finger at me. "You will accept a gift from one of us today, or no shower."

"Ignore him. You can shower free of obligation."

"I'm a better catch, and as you well saw, I have a bigger dick." Mas grabs his length. I don't look.

Nar laughs. "In your dreams, boy. Goodbye."

Mas leaves, and Nar stands there, hands on his hips. "I advise you to walk away."

"Why?"

"Because I'm horny and wanna fuck."

"Why don't you let me shower and you go jerk off?"

He laughs again, which lifts his eyes at the corners. I smile. I can't remember the last time I smiled or laughed, and I feel both guilty and relieved I can still do both. I thought I would die in that dark hole and nobody would even notice other than Feli the next time he threw me food. But I'm alive, and that's better than rotting in a pit.

Nar extends a hand.

I take it, and he rips the pelt right off me before he pulls me right up against his body. I look around, conscious we're in public. Although nobody's watching, I'm still apprehensive, probably because his hardness rests on my belly, and he holds me at the small of my back.

"I'm gonna wash you, pet you a little," he says. One hand starts rinsing my hair, scrubbing my scalp. That feels nice.

Even I can smell the dirt, mud, and God knows what washing away down my back.

"Back in Kalia," Nar says, "we have oils and flowers we use for fragrance."

I nod, happy he just wants to talk. "We have shampoos and shower gels. Well, on Earth. On Mars, they dry shower."

"Mars?"

I nod. "A planet near Earth we've colonized."

"I hadn't realized your people are conquerors."

"Oh, we're not. We...um." I frown, unable to deny it. Are we a conquering race? We're always hungry for more land, more power, more alliances, and we've warped our belief system to the point where we can't even see what we've done to a planet like Joylius. In retrospect, we occupied Joylius and spun our occupation as helping the Joyliuns live better. Are they living better? We've urbanized most of the planet and "secured" the native animal life into conservatories. Snuffed from main media channels but still existing somewhere in our database are reports of shortened lifespans among the natives. Ouch. "Mars didn't have inhabitants prior to our colonization, so we didn't conquer anyone."

Nar rubs my shoulders, palms trailing over my spine, and even though the water is cold, his body warms me in more ways than one. I want to touch him. But I can't, because touching another species the way I want to touch him is taboo. Humans don't mingle with others. Nobody does that. "What's your planet called?" I ask to distract him. Or me.

Nar takes my palm and puts it over his shoulder. It's as if he knows my inappropriate thoughts, while I can't sense anything from him. White eyes reveal nothing, and I'm at a disadvantage because my dark brown, almost black eyes, I've been told, are easy to read. Most humans' eyes communicate something, and eye contact when pressed against a man like this makes everything more intimate.

"Nomra Prime," he says.

As his hands roam over my back, lower and lower yet, they slide over my bottom and squeeze, then lift me up so we're at eye level. The arousal that's been blossoming in my belly since last night turns into an ache. My channel pulses, needing that hard, long maleness between his legs.

"We will need to shower tomorrow and the day after." Mas's voice comes from the tent. "Fuck her already and be done with it."

Heat crawls up my face. I'm a tomato.

Nar's unaffected, though he places a rubber stopper over the water hole in the tank. I expect him to put me down, but he doesn't.

"You are never returning to Earth," he states.

"Jesus." I feel slapped. Tears gather in my eyes, and my chin quivers.

Nar nods. "Kalia, where I live, has four seasons, with beautiful summers. There are baths the size of this camp, with warm waters."

"Why are you telling me this?"

"You have to pick the winner. You understand that? If you pick me, you will have everything you wish for."

"I understand the unfortunate circumstance that's my life right now. Collared and leashed and at the mercy of a warrior-class species."

"Don't pretend as if your pussy doesn't weep for me."

I pinch my lips. "A pussy can't weep."

He puts me down and kneels before me to press his ear to my mound. "It's weeping now."

I try wiggling out of his hold, and he snaps his head up. Behind the white eyes, a bright color shows, and I clearly see a vertical pupil.

"Let me go."

He smirks and walks away, but throws over his shoulder, "I feel bad for your pussy."

Asshole.

When he disappears behind the tent, my hands fly to my neck, and for the millionth time, I try to unlatch the collar or at least the leash, and when I can't, I curse, looking around for a towel or a cloth or anything to dry myself with. My body starts shivering, and I run back into the tent, where the two males sit next to each other, clearly having a private conversation.

"Sorry." I step back out. My brother hated it if I burst into a room while we hosted an important guest. Oftentimes, he would talk business in our common room instead of his office, so interruptions were bound to happen. My brother always felt that the house we lived in was all for him, and my sister and I were just inhabitants, when, in fact, the house had been left to all three of us. We were supposed to sell it and split the money, but my brother found it more useful to have his sisters live with him. Or he just liked controlling us since no other woman in her right mind would marry an abusive asshole with anger issues.

"Female," Nar calls.

"Yes?" I answer from outside.

"What the fuck are you doing out there?"

"I…" I don't fucking know. My brother's conditioning runs deep. Spending time in Gur's hole gave me lots of time to reflect on my life and examine my existence thus far, including how my brother has "guided" my actions ever since Dad died. My dad was my champion, and I miss him. I kind of miss everyone now. I wish the alien didn't have to be so blunt telling me I'm never going back. Hearing it and knowing it aren't the same thing.

Nar opens the flap, an eyebrow raised.

I walk inside and head straight for the sacks, trying to

find a towel for my hair. Nothing but blankets and furs. I eye the other clothes that aren't mine and can't bring myself to wear them, so I walk to the bed and shrug on a pelt.

They stare at me.

I clear my throat. "Do you mind if I sit down?"

Nar's eyebrows shoot up.

Mas just looks confused.

When they don't answer, I pull up a stool and sit across from the two, crossing my legs.

Nar reaches into his pocket, pulls out a red thong, and waves it in the air. "Want your panties back?"

"Those aren't my panties." Something awful burns inside me, and I want to slap him. Here he spent a night with me while having another woman's panties in his pocket, and now he's taunting me with them.

It doesn't matter. It's not like I care. I look away, my face burning.

"What do you mean they're not your panties?" he asks.

"They're not mine. You have mixed up your women, Nar."

Nar clears his throat. "No."

"Yes."

"I know what this is," Mas says. "This is the moment where Nar loses the games."

"Shut up, Mas. I do not have *women*. I have one, and you are it."

"That's not entirely true, because she's not yours," Mas says.

Nar growls low in throat. "Go wait outside," Nar tells him.

"No fucking way."

"You should return them," I bite out. "Maybe her pussy also weeps for you."

"It doesn't," Nar says.

"Nar is winded in the brain. What he means to say right

now is that he found the panties inside a white pod, in this camp, along with medicine. Show her the medicine, Nar."

Nar pulls out strips of meds, which I recognize as the ones he was trying to show me yesterday on the platform. Those aren't my meds and those aren't my panties, and those weren't my clothes I wore yesterday, and if they're to be believed, they think all those things are mine. If they're mine, they can't be another woman's, and if they don't know about her, she still has a chance of hiding from them.

I stand and snatch the panties from his hand. "Fine, you got me." I extend a hand to take the meds.

Nar gives me one strip. "You'll get another one tomorrow."

"If I pick you as a winner?"

"Even if you don't," he says, eyes narrowed.

I wish I could read his stoic expression, wish I could believe he truly is a good man. Or a male. A male who would gift me something he thinks I need even if I picked another. But I don't know that. "I won't pick another."

"No matter what they bring back?" Mas asks.

I nod. "No matter."

Mas furrows his brow. "Why not?"

"Because she wants me, idiot."

Mas rolls his eyes. "Down, boy."

They lean in, expecting me to answer. "Because I want to make a deal."

"Name your terms," Nar says.

Beads of sweat accumulate on my forehead. I'm risking my life here. I have no idea if these males will go back to Gur and tell him everything, and even though they're from a different tribe, it means nothing when I don't know if I can trust them. "I want to return to my pod."

Nar's jaw shifts from left to right, reshaping his entire face.

I blink, and his face appears normal again. Maybe I'm going crazy imagining things.

"I said down, boy," Mas repeats.

"I will take you to your pod," Nar says.

"Great. That's all I want." I can send a distress signal. Get rescued. Done.

"Here's what I want," Nar says. "I want pups."

Mas nods. "A fair trade."

I frown. "You mean like puppies? Dogs? What?"

"Mm-hm."

"Sure. When I return, I can ship puppies to you. Somehow. We have lots of puppies on Earth, and they'd love it here in the open space and forest. Maybe not in the mud, though they do like to get dirty."

"Yeah," Nar says, but his smile doesn't reach his eyes. "You have no idea what I'm talking about, do you?"

"I'm trying to understand."

"I will clarify. I want unconditional and exclusive access to your pussy so that I may seed your womb. Once seeded, you carry the pups, and once they're born, you can leave."

"Okay, this is the weirdest conversation I've ever had. I don't carry pups. I carry babies."

"Whatever you want to call them, womankind, but I want them, and you will give them to me."

I bite my lip. "That seems like a lot to ask for pod access."

"Take it or leave it."

He's preying on me, taking advantage of my terrible situation. If I don't stay with him, then it'll be someone else, someone worse than him. Would another male treat me worse? I don't know. If he did, I'd be helpless to stop him. These males are larger, stronger, more...dangerous-looking than any other warrior-class aliens. I need leverage and have none. Tears gather in my eyes, and I swallow, trying not to cry.

Nar looks away. "Take it or leave it, female." He stands and lifts the tent's flap to see the sky. "It's gonna rain."

I wipe tears from my cheeks. "It's always raining."

"Actually," Mas says, "it's not always raining. It's been raining nonstop for spans now, and while rain isn't unusual in these parts, rain with vicious thunder for this many spans is unusual."

Nar snaps his head to Mas. "Mae or Aoa or both are here."

Mas stares at me, a strange look on his face.

"What?" I ask. "Who are they?"

"Goddesses."

Creepy. "Should we sacrifice something and make them go away?"

Nar tilts his head. "Is that what you want? A sacrifice?"

"I'm just wondering what's the custom or ritual or… I don't really know. We only have one god."

"You worship a male?"

"Most think of God as male, but it's a spiritual being."

"You worship a male," Nar concludes and wags his eyebrows. "Come along, then. The games await."

CHAPTER ELEVEN

NAR

Dressed in blue pants and a new shirt under three furs, the goddess walks in front of us barefoot, her leash in her hand. Most males have made their way to the platform already, but the ones who stayed in camp whistle at her, making me want to bite their heads off. I sear them with my gaze instead, making a mental list of potential sacrifices, though if Mae wants them all as sacrifices, she won't need to ask me. She'll burn through this camp all on her own.

Mas nudges my elbow and whispers, looking around for eavesdroppers, "Securing a win wasn't smart. Gur will target you if you win, and me by association."

The shouting from a group of males doing an ongoing training on the left provides cover for our conversation. "You scared?"

"Of six hundred hunters against two? That's certain death."

"It's not six hundred. Don't be dramatic."

"You haven't seen what's coming."

"What's coming?" I stop to hear him out.

Mas stops too, and wipes his face. The rain has picked up again. "Lor plus two hundred."

Lor is the neighboring ruler Gur separated from when Ark gave Gur a piece of land, thereby making him an earl. "Is that what you did last night?"

Mas nods. "Reconnaissance. And what did you do?"

I push him, and his feet dance as he slips in mud.

Mas laughs. "Hookhole."

We keep walking toward the platform. "How long till they get here?"

"At the current pace, two spans."

At the end of the games. "Gur timed their arrival for the night of the endgame, when we know the winner."

"Maybe that's when he plans to break the truce," Mas offers, a hand at the back of his neck, head down so I know he's thinking. "If you were to break the truce, how would you do it?"

"Provoke Gur so he does it first."

Mas grunts an affirmative. "How would you provoke him?"

I purse my lips. "Win his games."

Mas nods. "Then you win."

I chuckle. "I thought we weren't gonna win or even compete?"

"You changed your mind, so I have to adjust the plan. You secured a win, so now you need to secure a way to provoke him so you can kill him, preferably quietly, though I don't believe that's an option anymore."

"Risky business," I conclude. Killing Gur out in the open could make the entire Ra tribe come after the Ka again, though we have some leverage inside the Ra. Ark, their tribal Alpha, asked for the kill.

"Any more rain and we're gonna sink," Mas says as we

reach the platform. The female stands before the steps, seemingly unwilling to climb. That makes two of us.

I bend to whisper in her ear. "You and I made a pact. I will honor my end."

She nods.

"You can't accept anything from anyone. Not food, not water, not shelter. Nothing."

"Got it."

I turn her by her shoulders to face me. "At sundown, if I'm not back and Mas returns, you go with him."

"Why wouldn't you return?"

"Because I'm dead."

Her eyes widen. "Are these games deadly?"

"Not always, but they will be today."

"And if neither of you returns?"

"You do what you must…and sit by the fire. Mae will take care of you."

"The goddess?"

"Of fire and lies."

Soaked and sad, the female takes a seat at the platform, and something in my chest tightens. I dislike seeing her unhappy. I dislike forcing her hand to accept my seed, but I can't back down either. I cannot let the Ra control the females. It's a death sentence for my tribe. We have to breed young, and we must do so soon. My brother knows this, and damn him for marking the one at home. A goddess, no less, tied to him forever so she can't breed with anyone else.

What he's done is tempting. Very tempting. I imagine the thrill of having a female all to myself. Marked and mine, only mine. Selfish of me to want to mark one. I shouldn't even be thinking about it. I shake my head, as if it will shake off my thoughts.

Mas grabs my belt and practically drags me over to the side.

His gaze is on Feli as Feli manipulates the portal controls, and I'm sure Mas is thinking what I'm thinking, because his hunter rises to the surface, making his jaw expand, making my skin itch, my hunter also rising to the challenge. Feli set up only five portals for ninety-three males. This means they plan to herd us, forcing Mas and me into a small area where they can surround and defeat us easily.

Feli nods at someone behind us, and I turn to see a group of Gur's males. Before the starting whistle sounds, a portal pops open, and the group rushes at us, pushing Mas inside. I crouch to leap after him, then freeze as the portal closes.

Cheating motherfuckers! Feli played us. They fucking separated us. I snap my head toward Feli, who whistles, announcing the start, never mind that they forced Mas into a portal before the whistle. The remaining four portals gleam open, and about fifty males, their skins all stretching, bones moving, readying their hunters to pounce, start circling me. My feet sink into the ground, so I step back, trying to find a firmer position. Their boots are also sinking. We can't stay on this terrain much longer, and I can't make the first move. They'll all follow me into the portal of my choosing, probably a dead end where they can corner me and kill me.

Gur designed the games to kill us. We knew this going in, and when I won the night with the female, I wounded Gur's pride and thereby his reputation among his males. Or, wait, not his males. The ones circling me *aren't* his males. These males came to him from another tribe. There are many Ra subtribes, and they wage territorial wars with each other more than they wage them against the Ka. Though they war with our tribe as well, a territory grab will unite them against the same enemy.

That's it. That's what Gur wants. United Ra. It's the same thing Ark, the Ra Alpha, wants, except Ark wants peace and this earl wants war. He won't risk his males to start one, though. He assigned the subtribe to me so if they kill me, Gur won't be blamed.

The viscous mud reaches my ankles. I lift my left foot, then my right, deciding I'm not going into any of the four portals. Mas isn't in any of them. He's alone somewhere, trying to figure out how to beat the other half of this subtribe. They look like southerners, maybe Ra long-hair, maybe not. I can't tell until I see their hunter, and I'm not provoking them. If I do, I'm dead.

"The games," I shout, "had a false start."

They boo me. I push through a group of males blocking my way to the platform. I force my hunter to the surface so they can smell his dominance. A good number of them step back in submission of the scent my hunter emits, and the aggression they smell makes their hunters uneasy. But not all move aside for me. A few males remain in my path. Nine, to be exact, and I sigh, annoyed that so many hunters feel equal to mine. They probably are, and that's even more annoying. Hunters don't suffer from false modesty or false superiority. They honor their instinct.

"A false start has to be corrected," I say, watching Gur up there while he stands with his hands crossed over his chest as if he has not a care in the world.

"Nobody here saw a false start," Gur says.

"I did," the female says.

What the fuck is she doing? I give her a pointed look, hoping she'll sit and be quiet, but no. She continues, "William L. Marcy said, 'To the victor belong the spoils.' Is that not what these games are?"

"That's right," Gur says.

"Where I come from, the games are fair because only with fairness can there be a true winner."

Gur walks toward her, his arm lifted as if he intends to strike her. I head toward him, but the subtribe males form a living wall and push me back. I slip, nearly falling on my ass. Straightening, I snarl.

The female stares at Gur, seemingly unafraid, but her small fists are clenched at her sides. "I can accept anyone's gift. Isn't that right, Feli?"

"That's right."

"I refuse to participate in an unfair game. I will give pups to the winner, not a cheater."

Gur swings.

The sky clears, and a firelight bolt strikes his arm. The bolt sears a path from the top of his hand to his shoulder and sets the fur he's wearing on fire. He screams and dances, shaking off the fur. He throws it and stomps on it, putting out the fire. Smoke rises, and with it the scent of burned hunter flesh, one we associate with Aoa, for she burned the camp of the males who tried to avenge her father's death.

As one, we all lift our noses and inhale the prayer smoke, letting the spirit of the goddess into our bodies. I close my eyes, enjoying the moment of the divine brushing my hunter.

A whine escapes Gur's chest, and I snap my eyes open. Whispers of Aoa surround me while the female stands there with her hands covering her mouth. The gesture reminds me of Stephanie, the human who enthralled my brother. She covered her mouth like this after she ate Sor's flesh. Cute human females, carrying our fierce goddesses inside them.

Feli pats the female's head and whispers something in her ear.

I grind my teeth. I am so annoyed, I wanna rip him to pieces. I growl at the pair of them.

The female sits down, and Feli returns to the controls.

Gur holds his charred arm, his eyes ablaze. "Kill him," he grits past clenched teeth.

Nobody moves.

"Kill him!" he repeats, then takes out his ax, bends at the knee, and throws.

I don't dodge the incoming weapon aimed at my head. Instead, I snatch a male next to me and force him in front of me, then bend. The ax hits the male's forehead, splitting his head wide open. It appears that Gur missed and hit the male, which isn't my fault. The subtribe won't tolerate a provocation like this. Bonus points for me if he's someone's brother or father or cousin. Revenge must be served.

A male in front of me turns from the platform and cries out. He drops to his knees, shaking the dead male on the ground. "Ore. Ore. Ore!" he calls.

Ore's head hangs back as the male scoops him up to hug him, blazing silver eyes locked with mine. Just when I think he'll attack me, he spins and leaps, his hunter pushing forward midleap. Gur's hunter responds and meets him halfway. They clash in a flurry of long claws and sharp teeth. The female is screaming, running toward Feli, who hides her behind his body. Gur's males rush from the training field, and the subtribe surges forward, war cries vibrating their chests right before they attack.

Males fight all around me, and I stand there sinking into the mud, staring at my female and the male who, by all accounts, protects her. I'm rationalizing why she would run to him and not to me for protection, and even though I understand I'm standing in the middle of a fighting pit, making her choice of Feli a wiser and more sane decision, I am offended…and hurt. I think she hurt my fucking feelings. I didn't even know I had feelings.

I push my way through the battlefield and climb onto the platform. Feli reaches for his ax. "Don't even think about it," he says.

"Think about what?"

"Taking the female."

"Your games are over. Gur started a conflict with a subtribe. You and I both know this won't be resolved for a long time, and the female is in danger if she stays in the camp."

"She's staying with me."

"Over my hunter's tooth, Feli. Move away." I allow my hunter to push forward, claws extending, jaw expanding, and I show him my teeth.

"Predator!" The female spins on her little foot and bolts.

My hunter sees prey on the run, and it's over. He breaks through and guns after her.

CHAPTER TWELVE

MICHELLE

My feet keep slipping over the mud as I sprint as fast as I can, trying not to fall, searching wildly for a way out of the camp. Huge creepy creatures from nightmares run past me, along with males in their bipedal form, their fight over at the platform.

What the hell happened?

One minute, I was a prize in a competition, the next, a meal amid the throng of alien predators. This entire time, I believed they were warriors, a class we could ally with, and my brother would love to ally with these guys. They're built for fighting and hand-to-hand combat, and the Martians would tremble in their wake should they ever decide to over-throw Earth's rule.

I reach the forested area, almost out of the camp. Yes! Seeing the goal line makes me redouble my effort. I run into something, bounce off as if I hit a wall, land on my ass, then scoot back as I see a creature advancing. Another creature jumps over me, and I duck, covering my head. I hear tearing, a yelp, and then silence.

I'm afraid to look up, so I don't. Predators prey on

humans, and I don't want to face one. I pray it will finish me off quickly, not painfully. Slowly sinking into the mud, I rock in place.

Something tugs on my fur.

I peek through my fingers. With no lips over the teeth, it leaves them exposed so the first thing I note is flesh stuck between the gaps and blood on the dark gums. The creature is the size of a horse, with a coarse, dark brown, almost black coat and large ears that stick out and make him appear even bigger. The sounds he emits are those of...of a tiger. A purring tiger, although tigers can't purr.

No matter how pretty I think tigers are, I would never pet one. And I would never want to face one either, though I think it's the better of the two options. This creature comes from nightmares.

He captures my fur between his teeth and tugs again.

I'm sinking deeper and deeper, and I can't get up. My body won't move. I'm so afraid, I might pee myself. Maybe I already have and don't even know it.

The creature rolls his eyes. I recognize that roll, the one that makes his head move in a circle. It's Nar. But I can't be sure.

"Nar?" I whisper.

The creature nods, then snaps his head up. His ears fold back, and he growls from deep in his chest.

It's a terrifying gurgling sound. I'm going to die out here.

Nar looks down at me and jerks at my fur again.

He wants me to get up, I think. I crawl out of the hole where I sat, covered in mud, and stand beside him, my knees shaking violently. Another one of these creatures faces him, and from the scraps of clothing that remain, I recognize Feli's kilt. He's so large that the kilt stays off the ground and doesn't seem to impede his movement while he's in his animal form. I've never seen anything like these males. Sure, we've heard of predator species, but they're rare and they've never breached our space. We've never seen one on the news either. They're the stuff of legends, an imaginary threat now made real.

Nar's tail brushes my leg, then snaps like a whip onto his back.

He does this twice.

The second time, he also lowers his body.

More males gather behind Feli, and I think Nar wants to get out of here, but he won't leave me. Which means I have to ride him out, and fast, before more males realize he's taking off with me while the fighting continues on the other side of the camp.

Oh God, help me. I straddle him like one might straddle a horse, and he rises. On top of his broad back, I wobble, then lock my knees around him and wind my leash around his neck. He tries shaking it off. I don't think he likes it, and I take perverse pleasure in that. I can't risk falling off him, and maybe the leash will give me more leverage.

Slowly, he backpedals. Seven males appear to want to chase him the second he breaks into a sprint. And I know he'll break into a sprint. What else can he do with a woman traveling on him? I plaster my body against his back, lock my legs around him even tighter, and hang on to the leash we now share.

He spins quickly, and I scream, nearly falling off. Taking off like a thoroughbred at the Kentucky Derby, he gallops, sometimes executing impossible leaps, making me feel like we're flying through the air. His speed is unbelievable. My eyes can't track the surroundings; everything passes in a blur, and soon, tears from the wind gather in my eyes, and I barely see at all. I wipe my right eye on my shoulder and try to look up and past him, but see nothing but his massive head.

There's a cut behind his ear running along the back of his neck.

I wipe my left eye on my left shoulder and look again.

The cut looks smaller now.

As I stare, it closes before my eyes.

Oh my God, a predator species with self-healing. My brother would kill for this information. They'd want one of these males in the labs. Self-healing is the most coveted technology on Earth. We can do almost anything, but we can't eradicate all disease, and we definitely can't heal our own wounds. Although we age more slowly than we used to, we still want to look in our twenties when we hit fifty. This male's biology would advance Earth tech over that of Mars. It would be our upper hand in negotiations, our superiority.

Nar slows and stops. A sting hits my ass cheek. It's not painful, but still, ouch. I think he whipped me with his tail. I look behind me and see nobody following, so he must have lost them. Thank God. Climbing off, I suppress a groan. My entire body hurts from being pressed against him for what feels like an hour. My collarbone hurts from bouncing on top of his hard back. Riding him any longer would shatter my bones.

The creature sits back on his hind legs, which fold like a frog's, and as I watch, under his skin, muscles shrink, bones move, and suddenly, Nar stands before me nude. He wipes his bloody mouth and spits flesh out.

Bile rises in my throat. There's no stopping it. Turning, I bend and vomit once, gagging until the reflux subsides.

I rest my palms on my knees. "You're a predator."

"I am. And you are Aoa." He grabs my wrist and turns my hand palm up. He unsnaps a golden bead from his hair and puts it in my palm. "There ya go, Aoa."

"It's Michelle."

"Not around here. Leave that girl back where you came from. Aoa will take care of you here."

"The goddess?"

"Of thunder and pain."

I scrub my face, unsure what to make of him or his goddess. "What happens now?"

"Good question." He chuckles and turns away, his hand flying through the air the same way Feli's had done on the platform. He seems absorbed in the activity, frowning, pursing his lips, so I know he's working on something I can't see. I look around. We're in the middle of a thick forest, and with no sign of anyone, I think we made it somewhere safe. Bugs are buzzing all around us. I hear running water nearby. "Are we near a river?" I ask.

"Yes."

"Do you think I can wash up?"

"No."

"Okay, so I should shut up and leave you to it."

"Yes."

Minutes later, I'm getting antsy. I move away from him, skulking behind the trees, looking out for the males who chased us or anything else that might spring out of nowhere and eat us. Or me, to be precise, since I doubt anything on this planet can eat this male.

The forest is eerily quiet now. Even the bugs have gone silent. "You're the ultimate predator of this planet. Is that right?"

"Yes. Where are you going?"

"Oh, I was...looking to make sure nobody caught up. What are you doing?"

"I'm reconfiguring the portal."

"The what?"

"The portal."

Holy shit, they have portals. A seemingly primitive alien

race, practically Vikings in space, have portals and miraculous healing properties.

Nar steps to the side and reveals a spatial opening. On the other side is a dark gap. Fear of being placed inside another hole grips me and makes my feet move. I spin and start running, but he's on me in a second, snatching me around the waist. I scream when he leaps into the void.

CHAPTER THIRTEEN

MICHELLE

I'm kicking and screaming when Nar throws me onto something soft. It's a bed, and I scoot as far back from him as possible, then fall off, hitting the floor. Gasping for air, I stay down, looking around, blinking rapidly, trying to get my eyes to adjust to the darkness.

I hear him moving around, his boots sloshing on the floor. Tiny lights ignite on the wall next to me, and I crawl away from them, but stay behind the bed as if it offers me a barrier. He's on the other side, his footsteps seeming farther away. When he stops, I hold my breath, heart thudding in my ears.

"What is this place?" I ask.

"My chambers. You can come out from behind the bed."

I peek over the mattress to see him leaning against the wall near a thick black curtain with gold and purple designs. The quilted work is beautiful. The walls are all painted yellow, blue, purple, and gold, and the tiny lights imbedded in the walls make me feel like an ant inside an artist's vase.

I glance at Nar, and when he doesn't make a move, not

even to cross his arms over his chest, I crawl around the bed, then slowly stand so as not to provoke him into pouncing.

He smirks. "Female, if you think I'm gonna hurt you, you couldn't be more wrong. But if you keep crawling around my room, I'm definitely going to mount you. Let's take that leash and collar off so I'm not that tempted."

"Good idea."

"I'm fucking full of good ideas of late." He points behind me. "The weapons are through there. Use a knife with a red handle."

I turn but see nothing. "Where?"

"Right in front of you."

"I only see the wall, Nar."

I glance back at him to see he's got this heated look. "My name has never sounded better. The *r* sound made from your tongue movement is quite sexy." Nar moves toward me, and I ball my hands into fists to stand my ground and not scoot into the nearest corner and beg for mercy. He's a dual-form alien, classified as predator, and predators predate on humans. I can't forget that.

Nar brushes my arm as he walks by, and I shiver. He sweeps his hand upward, and a lineup of clothes appears. He sifts through the garments hanging on an invisible rack. "If you find anything that fits, wear it." He bends at the waist, and because he's nude, my eyes find his ass, dimples on either side, and I've never seen a man ass as firm as his. His thighs are so powerful, the shifting of each muscle is visible, and I can't look away.

He turns, and I blink, then look up to see him smiling.

Caught red-handed, I feel heat crawling up my cheeks and know I'm blushing.

Nar twirls the knife in his hand and walks to me. He lifts my chin, puts the knife at the collar that surrounds my throat. I swallow.

He bends and pecks my lips. "For your information…" He kisses me again and purrs softly, making my entire body heat up. "The only reason I'm taking the leash and collar off is because Gur put it there. When I put it there, and I will put it there, you will crawl to me and do that thing you did last night where you put your mouth around my cock."

Cold metal touches my skin. He must have wedged the blade under the collar. His eyes brighten, becoming the eyes of the creature behind the pale white gaze. "The way you respond to me drives me mad. You fear me, and yet you are aroused by me. The mix of the two scents is as intoxicating as it is confusing. It's tearing me apart. I wanna eat and fuck at the same time." He slices through the collar. It and the leash both thump to the floor.

I gasp and step back, hand on my throat. Oh God, it feels like it's not my neck and this is some other girl experiencing the ordeal. I kick the collar away. Nar moves toward me, and I move back. His eyes blaze orange now. His vertically slit pupils frighten me. I keep backpedaling until I hit a wall, but he stalks me, pinning me against the wall.

"A cornered prey makes my hunter happy. A cornered *aroused* prey confuses him. I dislike confusion." He purrs louder and traces the side of my neck with his tongue.

"You can touch me," he says. "I think you want to. I think you want lots of things from me, goddess, or you wouldn't bother with a servant at all." His hand brushes my nipple, and I hitch a breath. He grabs my neck, squeezes. "I will not be your servant, Aoa. I will be your equal until the end of our time, not your time."

"My name is Michelle."

"Quiet, liar."

"It's on my birth certificate."

He bites my neck and purrs, stepping closer, his warm

body pressing against my front. I want to climb him like a fucking tree. Jesus! I put my palms over his chest and feel his muscles move as his hands grab my ass and lift me. "Take off your clothes."

I slide off the pelts he piled on me and unbutton the preppy white silk shirt that reminds me so much of things I'd wear at home. Nar sucks my left breast, now growling more than purring, and I dig my fingernails into his biceps. He leans his elbows on the walls, pinning me only with his body, and I start sliding down, detaching my breast from his mouth. Nar's eyes lock with mine as my body lowers and my pussy slides over his dick. He tore a hole in these jeans last night.

He closes his mouth over mine, and I open up for a kiss. He's pinned me, and I'm not moving anymore while we make out, him growling, me moaning. Nar's mouth and body feel like a fever, a fire, and I want to burn inside it.

Nar jerks his hips, and I hitch a breath while he kisses me. He jerks his hips again, and I hitch another breath. He's impossibly large and forcing himself inside me, and my channel clenches as he keeps breaching me deeper with these jerky movements. I lean my head against the wall and look up at him, intertwining my fingers at the back of his neck. Animal eyes watch me and make me feel like I'm doing something forbidden and deranged and devious for which my family would disown me instantly.

It makes me want to do it all the more.

Rebel against the constraints. Rebel against the norm. Rebel against the proprieties, expectations, and routes others choose for me that I never had the courage to rebel against alone. Nar, unlike me, is free and wild and uninhibited.

When he snarls, his dick jerks inside me. I lock my legs around his waist and let him fuck me any way he wants. It's hard and bruising and my back rubs against the wall, making me want to scream *freedom* at the top of my lungs.

Tears flow freely.

I want the leash.

I want the collar.

I want to crawl around his feet and beg to suck his cock, to swallow all the tasty seed.

Nar ruts, his pace fast, and when I come, I open my mouth to scream. He chokes the scream out of me, and I gasp for air as I keep coming, stars playing over my eyes.

He releases me, and I sigh, leaning my head back.

He's still fucking me.

I expect him to finish, come inside me, but he steps away. I slide down the wall because my knees won't hold me. Crumpled on the floor, I pant and wipe sweat off my forehead, blinking stars out of my vision. Nar is on all fours, his head lowered, gaze between my legs.

He reaches out and moves one of my knees, then the other, spreading my legs. Leaning forward, inches from my pussy, he sticks his tongue out and licks. His eyes widen, and he glances up before he licks again. He swallows and growls.

I spread my legs wider, holding my knees apart. I don't need to because he lies on his belly and uses his fingers to spread my pussy, thumb flicking over my clit. Nar buries his face between my legs and eats me like he's hungry, thoroughly, everywhere, even lapping at my back hole. Especially at my back hole.

I lift up on my arms and push against his face. He takes the hint and rims me, poking me with his tongue, and when he flicks it over my clit, my legs shake. He tilts his head and flicks my clit again.

My legs jerk, reflex making them want to close.

He forces my legs to stay open as he sucks my clit, drawing it between his lips, flicking it, torturing the poor small bud and me until I scream. He won't let me scream. He chokes me as I try, and this goes on for what feels like hours. I can't stop myself from grabbing fistfuls of his coarse dark hair and pushing him down, wanting him to devour me whole.

CHAPTER FOURTEEN

NAR

Fucking Aoa is like walking inside a fire: all-consuming, burning through my senses. My hunter rises to the surface along with the desire to release my hook inside her and mark her. My cock is painfully hard, hook swelling, readying to eject, and if I kept fucking her, I would have marked her.

Instead of fucking, I'm licking her, and the way she holds my hair and wants to suffocate me on her pussy makes me even more aggressive. I wanna fuck her until she can't walk anymore. It's almost as if I want to punish her for tasting this good. And she tastes delicious. This liquid, straight from the source, is unlike anything I've ever tasted. Sweet, but not too sweet. Tangy, but not sour. Perfectly edible to my sensitive palate. The more I lick, the more liquid comes, and I think I can do this for spans on end, even until the end of my time, a mere fraction of the goddess's time. And that won't do.

Snarling, I crouch and wipe my mouth. "Until the end of our time. Say it."

Aoa blinks as if awaking from a dream.

"Say it," I repeat.

"Say what?"

"What you're thinking." The goddesses trap males in their service until the end of the male's time, but they don't return the commitment. They move from male to male as they please. While some males share, I do not, and I never will. That's not what I want. I want her marked and mine and with me until the end of *our* time, which isn't the same as *my* time. I'm nobody's servant.

"I was thinking of..." She pauses to pull her legs against her chest. "Of what you're doing. Is everything okay?"

I lean in. My hunter mangles my voice when I say, "Aoa, if anything, you will serve me. You will breed with me and give me pups, and you will not be free to leave me or the pups." My hunter clouds my judgment. I just threatened to mark and trap a goddess. The loss of freedom would enrage her. She could strike at the entire tribe, and I'd be helpless against her wrath. How could this tiny prey carry a goddess within her? It cannot be true. And yet, she fucking owns me. I'm the collared one, and I can't stand it.

I peck her small nose because I scent fear again. "Don't be afraid."

She hugs her legs. "It's hard not to be."

"I'm a bitchhole. But I'm not gonna consume you." I'm not. Right? Yeah, I think so. Fuck. Dealing with a female is hard.

Standing, I extend a hand. She clasps it, and I pull her up, nearly flinging her across the room in the process. "You're light," I say, noting I need to learn how to handle her delicate, practically weightless body. When she rode my hunter, I barely felt her on my back.

I sniff her hair. "You must bathe. I must bathe. We brought Ra mud and dirt with us."

She huffs. "You didn't mind when you were eating my pussy."

"Oh, Aoa, I did not eat the pussy."

"Yeah, you did, Nar. That's what you did."

Horrified at the thought, I shake my head. "I would never eat that. We don't eat that part of prey."

Aoa's looking at me strangely. "Gross," she says.

"Exactly. I'm happy we agree on that." I carry her to the portal and open it, then step into the part of Ka land that has warm waters, and immediately regret that I chose this portal. At least fifty of my tribemates freeze, some midjump into the water, ending up plopping into it, emerging, and staring at my swollen hook and her in my arms. A female.

Tis recovers first. "Games!" He cheers like a lunatic. "We are having games again. Two in a row." Shouting commences, males cheering, arms up in the air, fists pumping. I turn around, bend, and show them all my ass.

"Boooo," they shout after me as I walk back into my house and close the portal behind me.

Aoa stares at me. "No bath?" she asks.

"Nah, we're good." I go to put her on the bed, then change my mind because if I put her on the bed, I'm gonna wanna mount her, and I can't do that because I wanna mark her, and marking her is a bad idea. Unless it's not bad. I haven't decided yet, so I walk to the sitting area and plop her on a stool, then check out the empty firepit.

I glance at her. "Can you start a fire? A small one to warm you up." Not a fire that burns the entire city. I don't mention her pyro tendencies woven through the legends of my people over the ages. Mae is her mother, after all.

Aoa shakes her head. "Were those other Ka males?"

"Mmhm." I need wood. I need clothes for her. I need shoes for her. I need bowls, vases, food.

Fuck, the food. "Are you hungry?" Thirsty? Horny?

"Yes."

Amti, the goddess my brother marked, ate the male Sor, and I'd feed Aoa a Ra if one were available, but none are, though they're coming. I stole a prize from their games. Just snatched her while they fought. I brought her into my tribe, and Hart's gonna lose his mind over what I've done. Eh, I don't wanna dwell on that now. Wood. Fire. Barbecue.

A knock on the door makes me groan. I just know it's my brother.

He knocks again.

"Someone is knocking," Aoa says.

"Yeah, I hear him."

"I would like to dress now."

I nod. "You know where the clothes are."

"I can't see portals, Nar."

"Why?"

She shrugs. "Don't know."

Groaning, I get up at the same time as my brother pounds on the door again. From the closet, I pick out a winter fur from an animal, not from a Ra. I don't need to provoke my brother when he's already gonna get all itchy under his skin when he sees a female in my house. I toss her the fur, and after she wraps it around her body, I open the door.

My brother Hart, the Kai of my people, the strongest, stealthiest, fiercest fighter in the lands, holds a bouquet of flowers and a bowl of soup. He looks...domestic and in a good mood, so I smile.

He shows me his teeth. "I'm going to kill you, Nar," he says and pushes past me. So not domestic.

At least two dozen males stand outside, leaning against the huts across the street, all bathed and perfectly clean, braiding their hair, preparing for the female they think they're gonna compete for. "Fucking traitors." I tell them. Hookholes couldn't give me a day with a female before ratting me out to my brother. I slam the door with a huff and follow Hart to the sitting space where Aoa stands as Hart walks up.

Her eyes dart from me to him.

"This is my brother, Hart, the Kai. Kai, meet…" I can't pronounce her name, so I say, "Aoa."

He sits down with his bowl and flowers. "Aoa," he repeats. "Goddess of thunder and pain. I'd say that's accurate. Thank you for gracing us with your presence."

So far so good. "Aoa struck a male with firelight. Burned his entire arm."

"Which male?" he asks.

I rub the back of my neck. "Gur."

"Ah." Hart's jaw clenches. "I take it he survived."

"Maybe. Maybe not, because the incident started a conflict between the Ra subtribes, so maybe he's dead."

Hart's lips flatten into a thin line. He might burst a brain cell from holding back his anger. Normally, this conversation wouldn't be as pleasant as it is, but since he lives with a delicate womankind, I believe he knows mine will fear him if he shows her his full charming personality. *Mine?* She's not mine to take. Fuck me.

"Where is Mas?" he asks.

I flinch, feeling like Hart just punched me in the face. I wish he had. "I don't know."

Hart's chest rises and falls as he controls his aggression. "Female." He addresses Aoa. She sits up straight, clutching the fur around her for dear life. I stand beside her and squeeze her shoulder. My brother notices the movement, a brief, almost lazy glide of his eyes.

"You must bathe," he says, sniffing.

Aoa chuckles. "I'm sorry if I smell bad to you all, but I've kind of been through a lot and kind of also gave up on pristine feminine appearances, silk suits, and French manicures. Excuse me while I go on acclimating to what I'm going through."

"You may use my bath, unless you prefer to bathe with the males. They will not hurt you."

I narrow my eyes. "She will use your bath."

Hart mumbles something, which I'm sure is a curse for the morning I was born, for I will likely cost him his precious peace. To be fair, *our* precious peace. If we wage another war, we won't survive. The Ka are just over one thousand males, and while we are resilient, clever, and strong, we can only sustain a few years of war, not a decade. Our wars are waged for decades. Hart wants peace. I do too, especially now that I have a chance at breeding pups. I shouldn't have snatched the female, and yet I don't regret it. I regret not taking Mas out of there too.

"She will use my bath while you and I have a chat." Hart stretches out his hands. "The soup tastes like chicken. I brought flowers in case you were unhappy, though I scent my brother has kept you happy in other ways. Bless him, Aoa, and give him strength. He'll need it."

I roll my eyes.

When Aoa doesn't take the gifts, Hart sets them near the firepit and walks to the portal controls, shuffles the screens around, and fixes a portal access from my room to his bath. The portal opens, and he sits back down, giving Aoa a kind smile, though I can sense that on the inside, he's fuming.

"Hurry up and eat." He nudges the bowl toward her.

"Maybe she's not hungry," I bark at the same time as Aoa reaches for the bowl.

She snatches her hands back.

"Oh no, pup, you can go ahead and eat." Hart smiles, and I note he keeps his lips covering the sharp edges of his teeth.

Hooker.

Aoa grabs the bowl and blows on the steam to cool off the soup before tasting. She sips, and her eyes widen. "Ooooo," she says. "This is delicious." She sips, then gulps, turning up the entire thing and finishing it off quickly. Once done, she makes a strange noise at the back of her throat and covers her mouth, cheeks becoming rosy. "Excuse me."

"You are excused," Hart says and stands, gesturing with his hand toward the open portal. "The bath?"

Aoa looks at me, and I nod, patting her shoulder. I never mentioned Kai's womankind to her because Aoa's mother, Mae, may hear of Amti and decide to take revenge. Mae and Amti don't get along and angry goddesses in one place awaken the goddess of doom, and nobody wants Aimea to awaken or find her place in the Ka tribe. Ark can have her.

Hart keeps the portal open after Aoa walks inside. She doesn't go to the bath but takes a turn and heads for a deep-green tent. I frown, having no idea why Hart set up a camp over there.

"It's a private wasting space," he explains.

Makes sense now.

Hart keeps the portal open as Aoa undresses. Since his back is turned to the portal, he doesn't see her nude body, but I do. My dick jumps in my verto as she bends to test the water and the pussy lips peeking from between her legs call to me. My mouth waters at the memory of her taste. Aoa's long silky black hair drifts across her back and over her shoulder. My vision sharpens. Even my hunter wants her, which is unnatural and something we don't do. Hunters hunt. Males fuck.

"Have you marked her?" Hart asks.

"Not yet," comes out of my mouth, and I snap my gaze to Hart, who's watching me with the eyes of his hunter. Aggression rolls off him in waves, and the scent of his dominant hunter pounds in my head, demanding submission. I glare at him, a low, barely audible growl threatening in my chest. He left the portal open on purpose, wanting to see how I'd react to her nudity, and now he knows that marking is on my mind.

Hart growls low and matches mine in tone and fierceness. I growl louder, my hunter disliking his imposition. Hart won't back down, so he rumbles loudly. If I as much as twitch my finger, he'll spring at me, and I wonder if he'll go for my throat. I've always submitted to my brother. He's the Kai, respected and feared, but he's challenging my hunter's instincts.

I gasp at the revelation. "The marking is the hunter's instinct."

Hart blinks, our standoff interrupted. "What?"

"The marking comes from the hunter. It's... It's an instinct."

"Don't make excuses for the marking."

"You marked."

"I did, and I don't regret it, but I'm the Kai."

I snort. "So I have to become the Kai to mark her. Is that what you're telling me?" To become the Kai of my tribe, I have to kill my brother or he has to die. After the natural death of a tribal leader, there are challenges, proceedings, and often games. "The strongest is always Alpha. He eats first. But when it comes to breeding, the games determine the winner."

"Which you didn't win, Nar. You saw an opportunity to take the female, and you took her."

"If you'd been there, you'd have done the same."

Hart leans in, practically spitting fire out of his eyes. "You left a male behind."

I flinch again. "They pushed him into a portal."

Hart sighs and scrubs his face, and when he looks up, he glares at me with pale eyes. "Tell me everything."

I recount how the Ra pushed Mas inside the portal before the whistle, and how I called out a false start, and how the female stood up and followed me. She struck at Gur when he tried to slap her, and it all spiraled out of control from there. Hart listens attentively, eating up my words, asking no questions, and I stand to pace as I talk, trying to conjure theories of where Mas might be, but my guessing won't help. "We need a location. He'll ping us via the portals."

"Veti is on the portals."

I nod. "Good. Good. Veti is good."

Hart stands too, my hunter making him restless. We walk around my sitting room, gazes on the floor, thinking of how this could all play out. I'm considering Aoa and what's best for her, while I'm certain he's thinking of our tribe and what's best for them. Snarling, I throw up my hands. "I am a selfish prick. A hooker. A bitchhole. But there's no stopping the marking. Tonight, I will either die or mark her. So either kill me or get out of my house so I can fuck her."

Hart marches up to me, his chest hitting mine. He grabs the back of my neck and yanks me to him. When he growls at my ear, I feel his breath on my neck, and my hunter rises, pushing against the skin, bones moving, muscles relaxing, preparing to kill. Instead of engaging my brother, I tilt my head while I still can, while I still have my wits about me.

A hunter can show submission in several ways. A neck is exposed when a hunter trusts that another hunter won't rip out his throat. I trust my brother won't, but he's also in a state of aggression such as I've rarely seen him in. He really wants peace, and I fucked that up for him.

Hart's quiet. Considering. I side-eye him.

He rubs his cheek against mine and steps back.

I roll my shoulders.

"When I marked Amti, I set a dangerous precedent for my tribe. I know that. But you don't have to. When the Ra kill themselves off, which could be happening right now, for all we know, Gur, or whoever comes out on top, will demand we return the female because the games must go on. We must return the female."

"Were you not listening? I'm not returning her, and I'm not competing. I will mark her tonight."

"And what about our males, hm? What of them? A single female can breed with anyone she wants. A goddess must remain free."

"Then have Amti breed someone."

He blinks. "Do you want to die?"

I laugh. "Do you?"

Hart sits, and I join him.

He leans his elbows on his knees. "We will blame Ark for this," he says.

I chuckle. Hart blames Ark for everything. Ark blames Hart for everything. The two predators have been playing the blame game with each other for as long as I can remember. "How?"

"He promised me females and never delivered, while I gave him access to the portals. Aoa should've been our female, as agreed to by Ark. We need to argue that there's unrest at Gur's camp and you fear for the females' safety too. While we argue all this, we can also sweeten the pot for Ark."

"Ark will never agree that Aoa was ours, and Gur is still alive." I don't ask how he'll sweeten the pot. The cost of my marking Aoa will only make my guilt stronger. It burns like poison in my belly as it is.

"I will pin Mas's disappearance on Ark," Hart says, every bit the Kai of my people. A ruthless manipulator in his fight to preserve his tribe and peace.

I leap out of the chair. "If we go that route and Mas is

dead, our males will seek revenge for his death. It'll mean war."

"Oh, brother, that's exactly what I'm going to avoid." He turns and heads for the door.

"Hart." I follow him. When he doesn't stop, I grab his shoulder and spin him around.

He clutches my head and forces our foreheads together. "Mas is presumed dead until he reaches out. We will watch and monitor for a decade, if that's what it takes. But for now, we move on as if we lost him to the Ra. They owe us a male, and if Ark wants to preserve the peace, he will have to relent on the female. The games are supposed to be fair, and they weren't. A false start is unfair and should've been rejected by the game master. Who was it, by the way?"

"Feli."

"The boy?"

"He's not a boy anymore."

"Hmmm. What is his position on the peace between our tribes?"

"I don't know. What are you thinking?"

"How I can leverage him."

"I hate politics," I tell him.

"Which is why I'm the Kai."

Goddess, my brother can really rub it in my face, all while remaining as pleasant as a hearty meal. "You hungry?" I ask.

He nods.

"Gonna hunt you something nice," I tell him. "You want?"

"I want."

"Thank you, brother."

"I'm leaving now before I bite you." At the door, he turns. "The females don't appear to see the portals."

"I know." I scrub the back of my neck. "Is Amti pregnant?"

He looks up at the sky and purses his lips. "It's too early to tell."

We still have no idea if we can actually breed the females. The wait is painful. What if they are just prey and we are fools? What if I mark a goddess and she has no intention of delivering me pups? What if Hart was wrong? What if Aimea comes and the war starts again? What if… What if…

CHAPTER FIFTEEN

MICHELLE

The water's hot, but not scalding my skin, and I hiss as I drop into it. Sighing, I cook a little, feeling my muscles finally relax, a sense of peace washing over my very soul. God knows I needed a bath. Those predators were so right.

The patter of the waterfall hitting the rocks and a bath in a pool that I'd call a small lake with therapeutic waters calms me. The scent of flowers and the small curious animals peeking between the bushes make this entire area a magical place. I can see why Hart picked it as his private bath. It's beautiful, and I could spend days tanning out here. I pause to consider. Days…weeks…months. Years. A lifetime with Nar. He thinks I'm a goddess and treats me like one. No man on Mars or Earth would compare. While I fear these predators, there's a lot about them and their Nomra Prime I like.

"Reminds me of Joylius in a way," a woman says in perfect English, and I startle and spin around.

A brunette with white eyes like Nar's and a kind smile stands by the bath. "Not the flora and fauna, but the atmosphere, you know." She carries a bundle of furs. "These are for you. I saved these for me, but they should fit." She places the furs on a clean rock, then removes a fur tube top she's wearing and unsnaps her mini kilt before jumping in.

She emerges in front of me, arms outstretched. "I want to hug you."

We hug, awkwardly at first because we're nude, but soon the familiarity of her soft skin feels almost as good as my mother's gentle caress from long ago. The woman squeezes me tighter. "It's okay not to feel okay," she says. "But you're going to be okay."

Tears gather in my eyes, and when she pulls back, I see she's touched too.

I cry freely. She dunks underwater as if to give me a minute.

Oof, I needed that hug.

Emerging once more, she swims toward the edge, and I follow.

"I'm Stephanie," she says.

"Michelle."

"They call me Amti, goddess of madness and lust."

"Aoa, goddess of thunder and pain."

Neither of us speaks for a while. We needn't say much. Strangers but not strangers to each other's circumstance, we have an opportunity to find solace in each other and what we've been through. "Where are you from?"

"San Diego," she says. "You?"

"Washington, DC."

We exchange small talk for few minutes. It feels like I met her at a gala and we're standing by the curtains, enjoying our champagne while crowd-watching. Stephanie is easy to talk to, words pouring out of her as if she's also missed having a girlfriend around. I always had my sister, though not as of late, since she grew bitter because of that one man who turned his attentions to me. She'll have him now. Hope he makes her happy.

Footsteps sound, and I look up. Nar's brother, Hart, is broad shouldered, impossibly huge, with black hair woven into complicated braids decorated with jewelry and feathers. He's tattooed, even on his face. The tattoo over his jaw makes me want to shrink into myself when he nods to me as a way of greeting. Luckily, that's all he does before he looks over at Stephanie and winks, giving her a knowing smile.

She blushes instantly, sinking a little under the water. Her white eyes find mine, and I quirk an eyebrow. She giggles. "That's Hart."

"I met him in Nar's room."

"So Nar won you in the games, then?"

I shake my head, unsure of what I can say to her. Hart and Nar together didn't exactly give me the warm fuzzies, and I can tell something isn't right about me being here.

Stephanie bites her lip. "Is Gur still alive?"

"Last time I saw him he was."

Stephanie nods. She appears as if she wants to tell me something and looks back at Hart, who stands by the firepit, watching her. When their eyes lock, he shakes his head, and I take that as a sign that Stephanie should keep quiet.

"Come on," she says. "Let's grab some beloys flowers. It's like shampoo and softens the hair. Smells amazing."

We swim toward where Hart's setting up a place to sit. There's thick cloths stacked over one chair that I think might be towels. Stephanie seems to have been here longer than I have. Her pale eyes tell me so. While she picks the flowers, I ask. "How come your eyes changed?"

"We think it's the hook. There isn't a way to know unless Nar marks you. Then we can know."

"Marks me how?" I accept the enormous purple-and-yellow flower and sniff while she rubs the petals until they dissolve into a partial liquid state in the palm of her hand.

"Their hook latches to the womb." She puts the flower juice on her hair almost like shampoo.

I do the same, and a potent, pleasant scent bursts in the air. Inhaling, I sigh and clean myself. "And?"

"The hook is how they mark the females."

"And how many females is that?"

"One," Hart says. "Just one." He's sitting by the pit, sharpening wood.

"For a lifetime?" I ask.

He nods.

That's all kinds of sexy. Hart doesn't seem like he's ever letting Steph go. As Hart does with Steph, Nar makes me feel like I'm not just a walking womb, and if that's the case, I better shut down my pod, because there's no way I'm leaving the signal out there. I've always wanted kids, and our National Security would hurt them. Oh no. At the thought, my hands stop massaging my scalp. My heart's beating a mile a minute.

Hart snaps his head my way. "What awkward thing is now happing with you, female?"

"I'm thinking about something."

"Can you stop?"

I nod. "Sure, yeah, no problem."

"Hart, I got this," Stephanie says and envelops me in a hug again. "It's okay. It is. We keep swimming. The current is in our favor. Their faith is in our favor. Whatever fate may come, evoke the goddess at will. They fear them."

Hart clears his throat. His hearing is excellent of course.

"Thank you," I say, and squeeze her, then continue bathing. "Are you going to have pups?" I ask.

"Oh, I'm having babies." She chuckles, white eyes lifting at the corners.

"How can you be sure?"

"Because that's what I'm having." She nods, looking

certain or, rather, determined, though I doubt she knows for sure.

"At least you won't lay eggs." Nar's voice comes from behind me, and I turn toward the bath entrance at the same time as he bends at the knees and leaps over the lake-sized bath.

I gape.

"It's the fitness," Stephanie whispers and waggles her eyebrows.

I drop my gaze and smile. It feels good to share naughty thoughts about another species with another woman. "I have so many questions." And thoughts. Thousands of thoughts.

"We have all the time to ask them. Let's dry off and eat."

Minutes later, the four of us sit around the firepit, Stephanie and Hart across from Nar and me. Nar's butchering something while I try to think of anything else. My pod, for example. "Did your pod get destroyed?" I ask Stephanie, who ties a towel around her body and sits next to Hart, legs spread before her and near the fire, toes wiggling.

"My pod is over at the tower." She points.

Hart's watching me like a panther might watch a rabbit. It's as if he knows what I'm thinking, and apparently he does, because he says, "Amti is staying here, Aoa."

"Of course." I nod.

"Do you know how to navigate the pods?" Stephanie asks.

Nar pauses midslice and turns toward me. "Do you?"

I struggle with what to say. I'll never see my pod if he finds out I can navigate it away from here. Pods fly on autopilot, but a licensed pilot can fly pods. "I have class B license."

"Oh," Stephanie says.

"What's that mean?" Nar asks me. "Why is it an 'oh' from the only other womankind here? Tell me." He hands me a dagger with thin-sliced red meat on it and captures my wrist.

He guides it over the fire, where the meat sizzles over the blade. My belly rumbles.

"It's unusual to have a class B license," Stephanie says, pale eyes locked with mine. "National Security clears those."

Hart leans his elbows on his knees and rips into half of the animal, the leg practically disappearing into his mouth.

"Go on, Aoa," Nar bites out. "We're familiar with your security detail, especially how they like to kill species classified as predators."

"I'm not National Security. I swear it."

"But?" Nar probes.

"But my brother heads National Security, and with it came the license."

"Oh my God, Mike the Snake is your brother?" Stephanie asks, eyes wide.

I nod, knowing what she must think of me. My brother, the Snake, double-crossing people and grabbing power wherever he can, me always standing by his side, smiling in approval, having no balls to confront him about anything even behind closed doors.

"Have you sent a distress signal?" Stephanie asks.

Hart leans in closer, practically ready to pounce on me. I glance at Nar, who's also leaning in, waiting for my answer.

I shake my head.

"Why not?" Nar asks.

"I couldn't. The tech crashed." I did try fixing the tech and almost succeeded. If they let me return to my pod, I could fix it now.

"As promised, I will take you to your pod," Nar says. "Or rather another pod, since I no longer believe the pod we found in Gur's village is yours."

"The meds?" Stephanie asks.

"Not mine," I say.

"What are they for?"

"I don't know."

Stephanie picks at her food. "Would you send a distress signal?"

I snort. "I wouldn't, but my brother would kill to get his hands on healing powers and portals." My heart thuds in my ears. Nar wanted a breeder, and the deal was he'd let me go. Trouble is, now, I'm not so sure I want to leave. When I set out to escape my brother, I never imagined I'd end up crashing on a planet filled with savages, but who said I wasn't allowed to like said savages? Or one in particular. I like Nar. A lot. He believes I'm a goddess, and his conviction makes me feels like one. He offers protection and safety. Freedom.

When I look at Stephanie and Hart, I want what they have. Their love is beautiful, and Nar and I... well, together, we can be beautiful in our own twisted way. I could live here with him and Stephanie and maybe even a few others. The ship destined for Joylius was full of humans. "There's another woman out there somewhere. We need to find her before Gur and the Ra do."

"If I asked you to pilot another pod on our land, would you?" Hart asks.

I nod.

Nar nudges my side. "Eat."

Nodding, I blow on the now-charred piece of meat on the blade and pick up a pair of wooden sticks Hart made while we bathed. I use the sticks to pick off my meat, like chopsticks. I eat quietly. Nar does too. Stephanie sighs. "Thank you, Michelle. You better than anyone knows how we treat alien species, especially predators with advanced healing and portals."

Hart grabs Stephanie's throat and turns her to him. He practically eats her mouth, purring loudly. It reminds me of how Nar grabs and kisses me. Even the kissing is predatory, as if they want to devour us.

Something wild and horny as fuck awakes inside me as I watch Hart and Stephanie. She strokes his thigh, and as he begins to purr, it reverberates through my body as if I'm her. Uncomfortable, I stare at my toes, then at Nar, who's watching me. I'm such an idiot. I thought he was watching them, but only I was doing that, which makes me even more embarrassed.

His nostrils flare. I know he smells my arousal. Nar takes my hand and leads me away from the bath and closes the portal behind us. The second we walk inside, he grabs my throat, squeezes, and I gasp at the orange in his eyes. Vertical pupils narrow into lines and make my heart beat faster.

I guess I'm always going to fear this side of him, but perhaps that's what I liked about him to begin with. "I fear you, you know."

"And I, you."

Nar kisses my lips, lingers. "I fear I will consume you, and it would kill me if I did that."

"I fear I'll come to love you, and it would mean destiny has brought us together after all. I considered staying on Joylius for good."

"Why?"

"To have the freedom to make my own choices."

"Were you thinking about running away?"

"Often."

"And now you have."

I nod. And I have a choice to make.

Nar kisses me while his hand on my throat grips me tighter and lifts. Pain arouses me more. Perhaps I like pain. Perhaps Aoa did come to me. Perhaps she gave me courage in the hole, courage to speak up for Nar on the platform and call a false start. Perhaps this is how this thing between us should be. Painfully arousing.

I stand on my toes. He sneaks a hand between my legs

and strokes my wet place, and as we make out, he pushes his fat finger between our connected lips. I taste my arousal and so does he. Purring, he walks us toward the bed. When the back of my knees hit the edge, I sit on the mattress and unsnap his kilt. His cock springs up, spurting some cum over my clothes.

It keeps leaking from the top, and I trace the hook over the tip, finding it hard.

Nar lifts my chin.

"Tonight, my hook is going to find your womb." He pushes a thumb between my lips, forcing my mouth open. With his other hand, he grabs his cock and shoves it into my mouth. Semen drips onto my tongue. Instead of sucking, I lick his hook like an ice-cream cone.

"You're a pretty pup. Prettiest in the lands, I think."

I smile.

"Go on and turn around."

I kneel on all fours on the bed.

Nar fists a hand in my hair and pulls. I grip his hand with both of mine as he pulls me into a kneeling position so that my bottom sits on my feet. At my ear, he says. "I said turn around, not get on all fours so I can mount you." He chuckles in that growly masculine way, and my insides twist. I start squirming on the bed, rubbing my pussy on the mattress. Nar doesn't let go of my hair. He yanks it so I'm looking up at him and bends to kiss me again, one hand parting the fur I'm wearing and touching my pussy.

I moan into his mouth as he strokes me. I hear how wet I am and moan louder when he inserts two fingers inside me. Shamelessly, I ride them, moving my hips back and forth while he's holding my hair and kissing me passionately. He smells like the forest, fur, and steel, and I can't get enough of how he handles my body. He controls me.

When he slaps my pussy, I yelp, also into his mouth.

He slaps it again, then grabs my breast and squeezes painfully.

I protest by trying to move his hand away, but he's holding my hair and still kissing me.

He grabs the other breast and growls as he squeezes it. I try moving his hand away because it hurts, but I notice I'm riding the bed at the same time.

Nar releases my hair and trails a claw up my arm, raising goose bumps in its wake. I try moving closer to him, but he grabs my throat and holds me in place. He pinches my clit, then pumps his fingers inside me, and I squirm on the bed while he holds the upper half of my body immobile.

"Please," I say.

"Shhh," he whispers at my ear. "Pups whine. They don't talk."

I hold his forearm and dig my fingernails into his skin. He presses his front to my back. It's warm and hard, and as he purrs while finger fucking me, my pussy contracts, and I come on his fingers, riding them until my body goes limp.

When he releases me, I plop onto the mattress, my vision blurry, my channel contracting with aftershocks. I can't utter a word or move. I want to stay like this forever. On the bed, with him doing whatever he wants with me.

And he does do whatever he wants.

"Look at the mess you made," he says, voice strangled, and if I turned my head, I know I'd see the scary hunter eyes watching me. I glance over my shoulder, and they shine like beacons in the dark as Nar licks his fingers, his gaze not on me but on my pussy, which is turned up and ready for him.

He swings and lands a slap on my ass. I yelp.

He smiles.

He lands another one and rubs with one hand while spanking me three times in the same place with the other hand. I cover my ass, a jerk reaction. Gathering both my wrists, he presses them at the small of my back, then climbs on the bed. He pins my upper body more, and I close my eyes as he enters me slowly. I'm so wet that he slides in entirely, and I feel his balls on my clit. When he doesn't move, I wiggle.

He groans.

I'm so full of cock that I spread my legs, practically doing a split on the bed.

He grabs my hips and lifts me back into the position he wants me in. And my pussy flutters.

"If you're a good pup, and I'm pleased with how you whine while I fuck you, I'll let you sleep with me. If not, you're going in the corner, and I'm gonna keep coming inside your mouth all night."

A shiver runs down my spine. His filthy mind turns me on. I feel free and wanton, and I wiggle again to make him groan and maybe entice him to lose a bit of control like I have. I'd let him do anything right now, especially when he's filled me with that massive cock of his.

Nar moves inside me, slow at first, and each glide inside me builds more fever in my lower belly. When he thrusts in earnest, picking up the pace, he starts snarling and growling, losing the soothing purr.

Holding me down, he ruts over me, and I moan, balling up my hands, my pussy slick and warm, letting him slide in and out as fast and hard as he likes. Nar releases my wrists and falls on top of me. He's still pumping into me and growling at my ear. I grab the back of his head and fist his hair. Lifting my head and opening my eyes, I sniff his cheek, lick it, then bite down and growl right back at him.

Nar freezes, then shudders. A jet of cum surges inside me, and my orgasm makes my body shake. I release his cheek and lie there on the bed, splayed, muscles relaxed. I'm like goo. Nar holds himself up on his elbows, looking straight ahead. I bit him so hard, there're teeth marks on his cheek. Jesus. I trace the marks with my finger, watching him so I can see how he feels about the bite.

"Do pups bite?" I ask, swallowing, a little apprehensive about the marks. I hadn't realized I bit him so hard. Blood wells up on his cheek from one tooth that pierced his skin. Horrified, I swipe the blood with my finger, and more wells up. I swipe again. He spanked me and choked me and all, and that's fine since he could tell I enjoyed that. It turned me on. I was aroused. But I have no idea if the bite turned him on...or off. "Say something."

He's still on top of me and inside me and looking straight at the wall.

He jerks his head up and looks at me with pale eyes. "What?" he asks, as if he didn't hear me.

"Say something," I repeat.

He opens his mouth, then shuts it, then clears his throat. "You marked my hunter."

I frown. "I did?"

"Pups don't bite grown hunters." He smiles. "But a goddess would."

He's being a good sport about the bite. "Should I apologize?"

"Not at all. My hook is inside you, and I won't be apologizing for that. I didn't ask permission, and therefore, neither should you." He retreats from me, and I sigh, feeling empty and missing his cock and body.

Fur hits the back of my thighs, and I startle. More furs pile on top of me. He's up and about, moving from bed to closet in seconds. I need to get used to his speed and the sudden movements he can execute so I'm not alarmed every time he moves in an inhuman way.

I flip to my back and curl up, seeking warmth under the furs. He's over by his closet, sorting through his clothes. A row of pelts and furs appears, and Nar pauses at one, stroking it. He removes it from the invisible rack and sits on the bed, shoulders slumped, head down.

There's something wrong. I feel his mood change.

I rise up on my knees and hug him from behind, effectively draping my body over his, leaning my cheek between his shoulder blades. "It's gonna be okay, Nar." I don't know what I'm saying, but I do know I have a tendency toward optimism, and sometimes with some people, that's what they need to hear. I needed to hear it from Stephanie, and I'm passing it on.

"You think so?" he asks.

"Yeah."

"A goddess would know, I guess."

"She would." I smile.

Nar strokes my arms with a claw, then moves up on the bed and covers me with the fur. I stare up at his face, but he's staring beyond me, maybe out the window, maybe just at the wall. I can't tell through the whiteness of his eyes.

"Is it something I did?" I ask.

"You're perfect, Aoa."

"Aoa is a nice name. Unusual and nice." And it's fitting that I'd change my name. Michelle seems like history. As if I left her on Earth. She wouldn't have survived this planet, not with all her proper and polite etiquette, a woman who's never been exposed to anything but luxury and money. Aoa, though… Aoa is kind of badass.

I didn't know I had it in me to survive that pit Gur put me in. I didn't know I had it in me to remain sane when he dragged me out on a leash in front of all those males or that one of those males would actually force me to wear that collar and leash and make me like it because he thought it was sexy. Michelle, the girl who lived under scrutiny of the media and her brother, wouldn't have survived. Or perhaps, I never gave the real me enough credit.

"I'm happy being Aoa-Michelle."

Nar strokes my head and sighs heavily, and I know he's carrying a burden on his chest. I wish he'd unload on me, but he's so hard, and unburdening his feelings just doesn't seem like something he'd do. Perhaps his brother could speak with him, or perhaps it's his brother who put the burden on Nar in the first place.

I close my eyes and move closer to him, seeking warmth and maybe even some otherworldly love.

CHAPTER SIXTEEN

NAR

I pat the fur over Aoa's body, feeling the peaks and valleys of her curves in the process. She's a thin female made thinner by the starvation Gur imposed upon her. Now that I've marked her, and she returned the marking, something not even the females of our species do, my mind drifts down memory lane straight to Mas.

I've known Mas for as long as I've known myself. I don't believe there's been a span when we weren't together, and there were times when I thought he might be a brother from a different mother, even though I know he's not. After the raid on my parents' house, Mas found Hart and me. He dug us out since the roof had fallen over our exit.

Over the turns, we battled many Ra together, always having each other's backs. Until recently. I failed him. I chose a female over him.

I grind my teeth so as not to snarl and wake up my goddess. I grip the fur Mas gifted me with after I saved his life that one horrible night when I thought his gut wound would never heal. But by then, he'd pioneered the first repair system on the planet and subjected himself to the test.

The males watched the agony he went through, and nobody would go near the repair system again. Except Hart. Because Hart's the Kai, and also a lunatic. Amti found her soul mate in him for sure. I am endlessly happy for my brother.

I leave the bed to stand in the middle of the room, pull up my portal control center, open a short portal, and walk into Mas's room, a small space with a bed inside the main tower. Mas never needed a hut, and our homes lay in ruins after the extended wars. I never asked why Mas never built a hut near mine. In fact, most males never rebuilt anything, expecting another war and more destruction, probably not wanting to bother with building anything when the Ra would just come and destroy it, and, yet again, we'd be forced to retreat deep into Ka territory to regroup so we could reclaim Kalia, this city and our capital, cursed to be located close to the Ra border.

Mas's room looks like Portal Central of our land. I don't believe even the tower portal control center has this many monitors or entries. I don't have access to his controls, so I can only see the maze of connections, bright golden lines and dots and stars everywhere. I swipe a palm over the controls, trying to open some portals here and there, but fail.

From the corner of my eye, I spot a fur from one of the vicious tribes living on Mount Omila. They rarely walk as males, more animals than rational beings. We kill them on sight, although sightings of them are rare. I run a hand over the fiery red fur, remembering this female. She tried to lure us into a trap and fell into a den of vipers herself. When they sucked her dry of blood, Mas and I snuck inside the den and stole her body. I removed her pelt and we burned the rest so when her people come looking, they couldn't scent us on her. We burned lots of land that span as we made our exit from that horrible place.

I unpin the fur from the wall and step back to see a strange portal, a tiny white light among all the other golden lights on this wall. Slinging the red pelt over my shoulder, I poke the portal with my finger. A net of at least a dozen portals over different parts of our land pops open in the room. And I recognize one, the same one Mas had set up inside the woods in Ra territory for when we needed a quick escape.

We've never entered from these locations, I'm certain of it. There's a portal even to Mount Omila, though none of us had ever returned there. Unless Mas has. I think he has, and I think he actually has access to portals all over our land. "You bloody genius," I say to nobody. Wherever he is, and if he's alive, he'll head for one of these places. I poke the portal entry for Gur's village, and as it lights up and starts opening, I close it.

I poke another portal on the other side of our sphere, and it opens too.

"Fuck." Mas granted me access to all these secret portals. I bet he thought I'd get stuck in one of them before he did. He's more cautious and calculating.

Mas is smart. He'd try communicating with me or Hart or the tower. He wouldn't think anyone would look inside his room. Or maybe he would. He ought to know I would come looking.

I sit on his bed and stare up at the ceiling. What the fuck? On the ceiling above me, a portal gapes open. Wherever this leads, it's nighttime, and I rile up my hunter and push him forward so I can see better through his eyes. Still, it's almost impossible to see where this leads, and as I try to ascertain this location, the portal shimmers, a sign of instability. I look to the wall and see the secret portal into Gur's camp shimmering as well. They're linked. But the ceiling portal is unstable. It can transport a male, maybe two at best, and then it's gonna collapse.

I bend at the knees and jump through it, landing on mud. When I turn, the portal shimmers, still holding. If I close it, it's gonna collapse, and if I don't close it, someone's gonna see it and come after me. I crouch and look around. Burning camp on my left. Mud under my bare feet. The smell of Ra fur and blood. I'm at the outskirts of Gur's camp. Fuck.

CHAPTER SEVENTEEN

MICHELLE

I awake with a jolt and sit up, fear coursing through me like a living thing. Through blurry, sleepy eyes, I see Nar jump up. I rub my eyes, look again. Um, what goes up must come down. That's the first rule of gravity, and they definitely have gravity on this planet or I wouldn't be sitting on the bed. "Nar?" I call out.

When he doesn't answer, I gather up the fur and secure it as best I can around my body, then walk up to the portal leading into someone's bedroom. Uneasiness makes me pause at the threshold. Why would he walk into another person's bedroom in the middle of the night? While there may not be any females around besides Stephanie, who is taken, there are males. Does this species swing both ways? I don't see why they wouldn't, and jealousy grips my chest, weighs heavily on me. Do I want to see what I'd rather unsee? No, I really don't.

I turn away from the portal and walk back to the bed, then think better of it and return. I curl my hands into balls. "Nar, I'm coming in," I announce. "And I'll rip your ears off!" I march into a vacant room. There's a single bed, smaller than the bed in Nar's room. There's not even a nightstand in here, and it's a small space but luckily, the dim lights allow me to see through an open portal.

It's a forest of some sort, and I stare at it, trying to jog my memory. I've seen this place before. I believe it's the portal Nar and I came through when we arrived in Ka territory. The one right outside Gur's camp. Has Nar gone back? Why else would he open this portal?

An insect the size of my thumb buzzes inside the room. Wait a second. If the insect can buzz in, that means random people can walk through it. Not people. Gur or one of the other predators. Something's wrong with that. Shit.

I wave my hand over the portal, but nothing changes. The image of the forest is sort of hazy, but I don't know what that means, if anything. What do I do? Just go back to bed and sleep it off, hope to God it's nothing, and Nar knows what he's doing? What if he's in trouble? What if he left this portal open by accident because something happened to him in this room? I mean, anything can happen to these aliens when they have spatial openings leading directly into their sleeping places. That's terribly unhealthy, in my opinion, but what the fuck do I know about any of this?

I spin on my heel and return to my bedroom, double-check that the fur is secured around my body, and open the door. On the street, the cold breeze makes the leaves dance in the air. A pair of males are walking up to me. They don't approach, but they stop and stare. One of them scratches his head. The other scratches his beard.

"Good evening," I say.

They nod in unison.

"I'm looking for Stephanie."

They keep staring. Two more males appear from around Nar's house and stop dead in their tracks. From up the street, a group of them walks my way, slowing down as they reach the house where I stand at the door not knowing what to do. The safest thing to do would be to get back inside the house and close the door and lock it. But I can't do that when something in my chest, almost like instinct, tells me I have to tell Stephanie, or actually Nar's brother, that Nar disappeared. If I'm an idiot for doing it, Hart will tell me or at least reassure me everything is fine.

"I'm looking for Stephanie," I repeat.

The males mumble, whispering among themselves.

"Damn it!" I stomp my foot.

The sky opens, and lightning strikes the door behind me. I scream and jump away as rain starts pouring as if someone opened a faucet. The males start shouting, and I think they're calling someone. A minute later, a figure dressed in an ominous black cloak limps down the street. He's leaning heavily on his staff, and as he walks, a bolt of lightning strikes the roof of the hut across from me. Fire ignites the roof. Oh my God. I cover my mouth as the males' shouting intensifies.

The black-clad male removes the hood of the cloak and stares up at this sky, then starts chanting and hitting his staff on the ground. I recognize my name, or rather the name Aoa, goddess of thunder and pain.

The lightning strikes the staff in an explosion of light and heat. The older male jerks and drops it, then staggers a few feet away from it. The staff turns black at the bottom, and sparks twinkle, then die under the pouring rain. I don't believe in their goddesses, but I admit, this is odd. Surely there's a perfectly scientific explanation for all this. The weather is unpredictable after all.

"Aoa, what has Nar done to wrong you?" the old male says.

"I'm just trying to locate Stephanie."

"Amti, Amti, Amti." He shakes his head vigorously.

"Yes, Amti. Where is she?"

The older male points at the tower down the street. I walk back inside and grab another pelt to hold over my head and then proceed down the street. Mud coats my feet and reminds me of Gur's camp and how he dragged me through it on a leash, celebrating the upcoming games. Fear makes me run faster toward the tower, and by the time I get to the bridge, I'm sprinting to get inside.

But the doors are closed. I pound on them. "Stephanie!" I call several times. The lights in the city are coming back on, air traffic stirring up. I had no idea they had air traffic. Various vehicles of strange shapes and sizes circle the tower while I keep banging on the door.

Something hard and warm meets my palm.

It's Hart's chest.

"Shit," I say. "I'm sorry. I was watching the traffic."

Clearly, Hart has just rolled out of bed, his hair everywhere besides tightly braided on his head. "What did he do this time?" he asks.

"I don't know, but he's not in the room. He went into another room. Maybe he went to his secret lover or maybe not."

"Not," Hart deadpans.

"Then I think he's in trouble."

Hart's lips pinch. "Show me." He marches down to the bridge, and I run to catch up to him and keep running because he starts jogging to Nar's house. The entire city is up, and males line the streets, strapping on their weapons. Hart pauses at Nar's door. While he barks orders at the males, I go inside.

He enters and closes the door. The second the door slams closed, Hart's nostrils flare. He shakes his hair and body like a dog might to get the water off, then walks across the room and right through the portal. I follow him into the other person's room.

"Whose place is this?" I ask.

"Mas's room in the tower."

Gaze on the shimmering open portal on the wall, Hart narrows his eyes.

"It's the portal in the forest we came through, isn't it?" I ask.

He nods. Hart's too quiet. I wish he wasn't. I wish he spoke all his thoughts right now so I don't feel like I'm pulling teeth when I ask him something. "What does it mean?'

"Which part?"

"Why is this portal open and fuzzy looking?"

"It's unstable."

"What's that mean?"

"Unsafe for travel."

"Oh no."

Hart grunts. "Tell me what you saw."

"Nar crouched on the bed and leapt. That's all."

Hart looks up, and so do I.

"Holy crap," I say.

"A divine waste is disturbing to me."

"We don't mean it that way." I point at the portal on the ceiling. "I know the outline of this sky. The curve of these five mountains. They're arranged in a shape of a bird. There's a belly, neck, and beak. Yes, I'm sure of it."

"How do you know it?"

"That's the view above the hole."

"What hole?"

"The hole Gur put me in."

"I hadn't realized you were in a hole."

I nod. "Yeah, before the games."

Hart shows me his teeth. "That male should die." His jaw

expands. "Nar went to finish the job." He curses. "The timing is wrong. He'll get caught."

"Oh no."

Hart moves his hands over something in the center of the room. He spends minutes there and keeps glancing up at the ceiling, where the opening's haze clears up a bit more. I think he's trying to stabilize the portal access.

"I don't see Nar," I say.

"Womankind doesn't see in the dark, that's why."

"I should see a silhouette of him out there at least."

"Unlikely. You are prey."

Damn. Okay, just lay it out for me, big dog.

A closet opens, and Hart grabs a sack from which weapons protrude, then walks by me, throwing over his shoulder, "Stay."

He crouches and turns, lifting an eyebrow. "I find that I have to repeat myself often with my Amti. When she understands and is clear on commands, she says, 'Yes, Alpha.'"

I salute the male. "Yes, Alpha."

He jumps and lands inside the other territory. A few seconds pass, and then he disappears.

I sit on the bed and bite my thumbnail, listening to the thunder and the rain pelting the windows. I don't want to lose Nar. He's my male. Overbearing and rough and all kinds of sexy. But mine. All mine.

CHAPTER EIGHTEEN

NAR

To my right, the males celebrate, and I wonder who came away the victor, Gur or the subtribe he invited into his territory so he can start another war. I snicker. He should've known better. The Ra are divided, each to their own subtribe, which made it easier for us to fight them in the wars. We prey on their divisions, and Hart uses them to kill each other off whenever he can. I can't say I'm sorry for either Gur or the subtribe.

They burned most of the camp, and the males sing and dance, going around setting the rest on fire. They're drowning in smoke. A Sha-male must've come, and now they're praying, likely calling a goddess, maybe even Mae, goddess of fire and lies. I shudder, not wanting to be anywhere near Mae.

The rain stopped with my goddess's departure, and I survey the camp, seeking Gur but I can't stay in one place for long because my feet are sinking into the mud. Behind me, I sense a male and spin, baring my teeth. Pale eyes like beacons shine in the night. The wind in my favor blows his scent toward me. It's my brother.

Hart trudges through the mud. Hands on his hips, he gives me his best annoyed look.

"Mas led me here," I say as an excuse for standing on enemy territory.

"By your hand, he led you here?"

My brother can be a sarcastic twat. "Via a hidden portal."

"That should've stayed hidden, Nar."

"You knew about it?"

Hart nods.

"Why didn't I know about it?"

"Because I'm the Kai. Let's get back."

"No fucking way. Gur could be alive."

"Leave him to Mas."

"Provided Mas is alive."

Hart nods.

"I have to look for him. You understand?"

Hart shakes his head.

"I don't need your permission," I say.

Hart grabs the back of my neck and pulls, slamming our chests together. "We're sinking in the mud in Ra territory," he says, "and you want to have a pissing match?"

I grind my teeth. "No, Alpha."

He pats my head and rubs his cheek against mine, reminding my hunter we're on the same side even when we disagree.

"Psst," comes from behind Hart.

He spins and crouches, and I crouch with him to see Michelle standing in the middle of the open field waving at us. What the fuck? I blink, not believing what I'm seeing.

"I told her to stay," Hart deadpans.

I tsk. "Womankind aren't trained."

"Then we must train them."

"Agreed."

We creep up to her, and she crouches too, whispering, "There's someone in my hole."

"What hole?" he asks while I glare, not wanting to speak because I'm so pissed she's here. The portal could've collapsed and cut her in half, and I don't believe all three of us can return the way we came.

I glance at the portal, which is barely visible now. "We have no time to chat, and I'll deal with you in private."

Michelle swallows. "Okay, but there's someone down there." She points at the ground, and it occurs to me we're no longer sinking. I dig under my feet and find wood. Hart starts digging too, and we discover an underground cage, a holding cell we use for hunters who need solitary confinement for whatever reason, most often when they can't find their way from berserk hunter back to male.

Michelle moves away and sinks almost to her ankles.

"Keep moving," I hiss. I am so upset that she would put her life on the line for me. It warms my heart, but it also makes me crazy that she left the safety of our home and territory, where males would've died protecting her in my absence.

Eyes trained on the camp and the line of fire spreading outward, Hart and I keep digging. There are a few unlit tents settled closer to our position, and I'm sure the Ra will make their way there either to sleep or to burn them down.

Once I find the cage latch, I nod at Hart, and we step away so I can open the lid. We peer inside. The hole is deep, with Mas sitting in shallow water at the bottom, orange hunter eyes staring up at us.

"Leave me," he says, voice mangled.

Hart snorts and digs into the sack he brought. He pulls out a rope. One end, he ties around his waist, while I get the other end and throw it to Mas. He leaves it dangling. When he won't climb up, I glance at the camp. Several Ra males are making their way to the tents near us. If they look past the camp, they'll see us, and then they're gonna hunt us.

"Aoa, get back into the bedroom," I say.

"Okay."

Hart nods. "Good girl."

I jerk the rope. "Mas, you can either tie it to yourself or I'll do it for you, because I'm not leaving you."

"Gur is alive, and I can take him down if you leave me in the hole." Mas lifts his feet out of the muddy water and shows us why he can't reach the rope. The hole is full of iron traps that bit into his feet. His ankles look crushed to the bone, and he can't stand. His hunter would heal faster, so I don't know why Mas isn't healing that way. He must have a reason.

I drop into the hole and grunt as my feet touch the bottom, which is reinforced with solid metal. I get the rope and slowly approach Mas. He snarls at me. I lean back and look away, not wanting to trigger his hunter's instincts. A wounded hunter is a dangerous predator.

"I said leave me." His voice tells me all I need to know. Mangled and gruff, it tells me Mas is somewhere deep into his head, half hunter, half male, a state I dislike for several reasons, one being a lack of clarity of thought. It's also the state I entered before I released my hook. In all my years, I never knew this state existed, which raises the question. "Did you find the other female?"

Mas doesn't answer. He doesn't have to. I know him better than I know myself. Mas isn't suicidal or stupid. He would have shouted for me to come and bail him out of the hole. He would have healed in hunter and found a way out. But if there's a female he's trying to win or protect...that changes his story as it changed mine.

I pull back my fist and sock him in the face.

Bones crunch, and Mas's head loops to the side. I tie the

rope around his waist and lift him, then look up and nod at Hart, who pulls hard. He slips, and I wince. If he falls in, all three of us are staying down here in the dark cold muck. It's five males deep with no way to climb up. And this is the hole Gur placed a human woman in. I don't know how Michelle survived the cold, the water, the hunger. Perhaps Aoa helped her. Perhaps womankind are stronger than they appear.

Hart finds a better position for his footing, and I can hear his muscles straining as he drags Mas out. A moment later, the rope drops for me, and I tie it around my waist. Hart hauls me out, and I pat him on the chest as he pants, barely able to catch his breath.

"Tired?" I ask.

He narrows his eyes.

I smile. Gotta love fucking with Hart. He takes everything so seriously.

"Let's get out of here." Hart focuses somewhere behind me, and I turn. A male is pissing at the back of a tent. He can't hear us because of the chattering of others inside the tent who are drunk on smoke and slurring their words, but if he turns his head even slightly, he'll spot us. Hart picks up Mas and settles him over my back, and we move toward the portal, even though we both know it won't be stable long enough for either of us to pass.

When we reach the portal, I throw Mas inside, landing him right on his bed. Sighing, I stare at Michelle, who's looking up from near the bed.

"Well, come on," she says.

Hart throws the sack into Mas's room. I drop my clothes in there too.

"What are you doing?" Michelle asks, terror evident on her face.

Shouting comes from the camp. They saw us. It was inevitable.

"Stay," I order her.

"No, Nar, you need to come back."

The portal shimmers, and I shove Hart inside. His shout rings in my ears, but I can't have the Kai of my people getting caught by two hundred and some hunters. He is a mighty fighter, but he's not that mighty, and two fighting against two hundred, as Mas so eloquently put it, is stupid.

My hunter takes over as I sprint toward the forest portal, hoping against all hope that the Ra haven't found it yet. At first, only a dozen males chase me, but as I sprint, the ground under my paws starts shaking as dozens more join the hunt.

I sense they're spreading out. They're gonna cut off my path to the forest, so they know where I'm going. I change direction and head for our border right across the river. It's either the river or over River Stones, and that's bad terrain to cross in the middle of the night.

As swiftly as I can, I gallop toward the river, Ra males closing in on me. I hear the water already, and I'm almost there. A hunter springs out of the river. It's a Ra hunter, a massive one, and I skip to my left trying to avoid him, but he's fast and runs right at me. I skip right, and he's there too.

Blazing silver eyes.

Gray-white hunter.

Ark.

The Ra close in on me, and with Ark in the front and many males at my back, I'm trapped. I snarl, my hunter hating being cornered. Ark shakes off the water and sits back on his hind legs, and his body convulses as he becomes a male. With a smirk, he sits down as if he's at a casual gathering. The conniving devious hookhole can't be trusted, so even if he's telling me he's not a threat, I know better. I remain a hunter, crouching, eyeing his jugular.

"Gur is dead," he says and remains sitting, even picking a piece of grass to stick in his mouth.

Lies. Mas said Gur lives, unless he's died while Mas was in the hole. I don't know, and I don't trust Ark.

Lightning cracks the sky. The coming storm gathers the dark clouds the way the predators gather on an open field. I glance past the river to the top of the hill that's controlled by the Ra. I almost made it. Our territory is right beyond it.

Ark looks up at the thunder flash, practically inviting me to rip out his throat. I am tempted. I am so tempted. Saliva gathers in my mouth, and I growl low in my throat.

"I hear the goddess has cursed Gur. The wound she inflicted festered and couldn't heal." Ark smirks. "You're stupid enough to return to my territory, so I think you should take the fall, seeing as how you snatched her, and, if your brother and father are any indication, you've also marked her by now. For which you should die. On my land."

He wanted Gur dead, but he can't say that in front of his males. I get it. But Ark has a plan, and my death will cost him a war, which he won't start. So he's playing at something. Better I stay in hunter and let him do all the yapping.

Ark jerks his head, then stands, wiping his hands and flicking the dirt under his claw. Past the river, up on the hill, my tribemates emerge and form a line, holding hostage the Ra males who patrol their border. There're hundreds of us, and my brother stands in the middle. He lifts his arm. If he drops it, the Ka will rush in and slaughter the Ra on the field. Which would be optimal, because I enjoy killing the Ra. But not so lovely for the family I intend to raise in peace.

Ark snarls. "Hart, stay where you are and release my males."

"My brother first," Hart says.

"I'm not stopping him."

Behind me, the Ra protest, shouting that I stole a female, but Ark snarls at them too.

"Do you want to die in your beds of festering wounds?

Hm?" He walks the lineup of his males, every bit an Alpha hunter, pounding them with his dominance, forcing Ra hunters to surrender to his will.

They fall silent. No male in the land wants to die in his bed.

"Leave the goddess to the Ka, I say," Ark shouts. "Let her destroy them from within."

At first, the males' murmurs tell me they're thinking about what Ark is saying. It takes them a beat to agree with him because he makes sense and because he's a conniving hookhole who tends to be good with words. Kind of like my brother.

Ark grunts and pats my head as he leaves. "Good boy."

I roll my eyes and cross the river, then walk up the hill on two feet. Aoa pushes her way through the males and jumps on me, hanging to my neck, demanding I hold her. I do. I hold her up, squeeze her ass, and slap it. "You're a bad pup."

She kisses me and sticks her tongue into my mouth, and we make out while the males boo me for snagging a female. A goddess of thunder and pain, no less. I'm such a hooker and regret nothing.

CHAPTER NINETEEN

MICHELLE

"Mae," the Sha-male says as he laces his wrinkled, clawed hands on his lap, "blamed Amti for Aoa's madness."

"Aoa was crazy?" I ask while I use a small ax as a hammer. Predators have no need for dining tables. They hunt in the wild and eat, only making provisions for us around the firepit and only because we eat our food cooked. Stephanie and I decided we'd make a small table. Actually, we have plans for putting up a gazebo near the baths.

"Amti is the mad one," he corrects. "Mae accused Amti of influencing Aoa to want to bed her father."

"Aoa slept with her dad?" I gape, nearly dropping the ax.

"And I'm the crazy one?" Stephanie says. "I think not." She sits next to me and leans back on her hands, gaze on the Sha-male. Getting him to talk to us took ten days. He's terrified of us, but we bribed him with a favor. We promised to get along, not call Aimea, goddess of doom, and we also swore to spiritually seek Mae, my goddess mother. The Sha-male believes Amti felt Mae walking among us, and that was why she cursed Ark. Stephanie is great, and we're friends, but spiritually seeking a goddess isn't something we can do, I'm afraid, even though we said we would. The Sha-male believes in us, though. They all do, and Stephanie and I, although acknowledging weird things happening with us (like lightning bolts hitting rooftops when I walk down the street), it's difficult for us to lose our own faith and accept another one. It doesn't, however, make their beliefs any less significant or meaningful.

"Then what happened?" I ask.

The Sha-male stands and walks to the wall, looks up, and points. "Here it is."

We can't read their alphabet yet. That's next on our list of *how to con Sha-male to reveal all their legends*. They're extensive, rich, and reveal a strong faith despite their technology. The disconnect between technology and their primitive behavior fascinates me. All this rich culture survived the test of time and technology, which is far more than I can say for humanity. We barely write by hand anymore, whereas the Sha-male paints walls, recording history so that thousands of years after he's gone, another Sha-male can tell the same stories he's telling us now. A thought occurs to me. "Are you recording what's happening as we talk?" I ask.

"Of course. It is why I've been so busy and have little time to spare for scripting events I've already written on the wall."

Stephanie chuckles. "He's politely telling us to learn how to read."

"After the gazebo."

"Priorities," she says and turns up her nose. She wiggles it in a human way, not in a predator way. Stephanie's senses have grown more acute lately. My eyes changed too, and now I can see the portals' golden lines. I navigate some, simple ones, mainly, but I'm determined to learn everything about them. Vacationing on another side of this planet at whim is a freedom unlike anything on Earth. My sense of smell should develop next. I'm very excited to be able to hear and smell when my mate is nearing home the way she can scent Hart.

I turn and spot Hart and Nar coming up the bridge. Standing, I wipe my hands together. "Thank you, Sha," I say, but he's already painting and waves me off. I stretch out my hand to help Stephanie stand, and she takes it, fixing her fur tube top once she's on her feet.

Hart marches inside the hall, Nar lingering at the door with another male.

"Caught an ored." Hart pats the deer-size, white-furred animal slung over his shoulder. Blood drips all over his clothes. I'll never get used to this, and apparently neither will Stephanie, because she bends at the waist and vomits on Hart's boots.

Bile rises in my throat, and I step away, looking anywhere besides his feet.

Hart stares at his boots.

Stephanie wipes her mouth. "I'm soooo sorry. It came out of nowhere."

Hart lifts his gaze. "No ored, then. Nar!"

Nar jogs inside and stands next to me, sneaking a hand under my skirt to grope my ass. I blush because I'll never get used to his public displays of affection either. It doesn't matter that these two people are my closest friends now. Nar's so sexy and dirty, and my thoughts, when he's around, are inappropriate. Some nights, he collars me and puts me in the corner, then spanks me, calling me a bad pup. I've never felt dirtier and sexier in my life. Most nights when we fuck, I don't know who's worshiping whom, but I do know I'm eager to hear if Stephanie is pregnant. The entire tribe awaits good news. They pray nightly. The Sha-male even suggested Mas should leave for some place inside Ra territory where Sha believes the Ra hold a captured Ka tribe Sha-male, a younger male who can handle all the rituals and scripting without tiring.

Stephanie walks back a few steps, looking pale and sickly. She plugs her nose, shaking her head. Hart catches on quickly. He slings the catch off his shoulder and pitches the animal toward Nar, who grunts at the impact.

"You eat it," he says to Nar and slowly stalks Stephanie until he's pinned her to the wall. I know I shouldn't think it, but I'm thinking it anyway. Hunters corner prey, and watching Hart corner her is like watching porn.

"What awkward thing is happening to you, Amti?" he asks. "I worry."

"I don't know, Hart, but the smell is making me sick. I need a bucket." She pushes his chest, bends, and vomits again.

Poor Stephanie. We've dined together since I arrived, and I'm fine. The ored scent is inoffensive to my nose, so… "I think you're pregnant," I announce. Lord, I hope I'm right.

The Sha-male turns.

Hart snaps his head my way. "Why do you think that?"

"Pregnant women get sick often in their first trimester. They're sensitive to smell and have nesting needs." Stephanie thought of the gazebo and tables, and I'm sure she'll ask for a nursery soon.

"Oh," Stephanie says. "She's right."

I jump up and down. "We're going to have puppies!"

"Girl, no, I'm having babies."

I rush to her and give her a hug before Hart can recover and snag her for the next eight months. I imagine how protective he'll get now that he's sure she's carrying his pups. "Sure" is a loose term. We don't have checkups here, ultrasounds, or anything of the sort, but a woman knows what she knows. And when I peel myself off Stephanie, she smiles and touches her belly.

I return to Nar, and we leave the couple with the stunned

139

Sha-male in the hall to walk back to our hut, Nar quieter than usual. When we enter, he pins me against the door, lifts my leg, and parts his verto. He enters me.

I'm dry.

It's painful, and I like it.

The back of my head hits the door, and my eyes roll to the back of my head. He palms my ass and growls, his hunter eyes showing. I fist his hair and yank to get his hunter riled up. He fucks me harder, my back scraping the door, and I lean forward and bite his cheek, knowing how much he likes this, knowing how it gets him off, and I take great pleasure in getting him off, making him lose some of that control he holds over his hunter.

"I'm going to have your puppies," I whisper at his ear.

Nar's growling, rutting into me.

"And I will strike down the tower if you don't destroy the pods like I asked you to." I gasp, shocked at my own words, but Nar's still fucking me as if he hadn't heard a thing. Perhaps I said nothing. Perhaps it was all in my head. Perhaps the goddess of madness and lust did influence Aoa, and I am indeed mad. But if I am to be mad, at least I will be madly in love with a predator who worships me.

***

Hi, Milana here. Thank you for reading Stolen, and moving through the Tribes series with me. I truly hope you loved Nar as much as I did. He's so dirty and possessive and his bedroom tastes are some of my favs. I also really loved his friendship with Mas, who is next in line for a book and you can read the preview on the next page.

LURED EXCLUSIVE TEASER

In the middle of the night, instead of sleeping and healing, bleary-eyed and mighty annoyed with my state of mind, I stare at my private portal controls. I hacked the portal control center Feli erected during the Ra games. All I have to do now is pull up the portal he shoved me into and step onto the sand just beyond the shimmering opening. I even packed my sack, strapped on weapons, and brought a gift I made during the cycle when I couldn't stop thinking about the footprints with ten small toes.

The fact I wanna find a female isn't unusual.

The fact I wanna go off to look for the female near the Blood Dunes is unusual.

It's unlike me to risk my life when I know I can't win. And when faced with a female who could be a goddess, a male cannot win. They have a way of crawling under the skin and wrapping their claws around our hunter's necks, stroking those instincts for both breeding and hunting, making us more predatory than we want to be, making us obsess over them and serve them till the end of our time.

Standing, I rub the back of my neck. If I tell Hart where

I'm going, he'll prohibit it. Or worse, send me in with a group of Ka males, risking their lives as well as mine in the process. We're just over one thousand males, and every male counts, or we'll be wiped from the face of the planet, become a historical swirl on a wall commemorating the Ra conquests.

Before I can talk myself out of this, I jump into the portal and land on the sand of the Blood Dunes. I don't linger. The moment my boots touch the sand, I sprint for the thick forests surrounding the Dunes on three sides. The North Dunes is nothing but sea.

My tracks. Crap. I walk back and scratch out my tracks with the ax and keep covering them, running backward, bent over and all kinds of awkward and slow. But I don't want the womankind (or goddess) to know I arrived. I need to catch her unawares, and I need an exiting portal inside the forest for that to happen. I am not going back on the damned sand where my ancestors lay bleeding for span after span, unable to heal, unable to die, while the goddess of blood and grace danced, hopping from body to body, evoking her favorite song made by the wheezing of their lungs beneath her perfect foot. With five small toes.

Leaping now, because I can't get the fuck out of there fast enough, I land on the rock and hop to another, then another, until I reach the upper part of the rock-strewn forest. Having safely made it past the sand, I settle between two boulders and get out the ritual stones and the wood. On the ground, I arrange them into the pattern that will signal a sacrifice to the goddess of blood and grace and then cut my palm with a knife, wincing at the pain. She's fond of bleeding predators.

I clench my fist so my blood drips over the wood and stones, then light a fire and snuff it out before the fire goddess, Mae, decides it's for her. Smoke rises, and I wave my hand to direct it toward me and inhale the body of Eme, goddess of blood and grace. *There ya go, female. Mas loves you. Fuck off now, and let me have the human sans your bloodthirsty spirit.*

I glance at the cut on my hand. It's not healing as quickly as usual. I stare at it, willing it to close up. Nothing. Good, this is good. It means I've done the ritual as the Sha-male instructed and not fucked it up. I'll recover soon.

Something zips past above me, and I duck. When I hear the whistle of it farther away, I lift my head.

A round white pod, much like the two pods I've secured on our main tower over in Kalia, lands on the sand. I perk up, anticipating my first view of the human female and inwardly congratulate myself on finding her. Who needs Ark to deliver females when they have Mas the portal master, hm? Gonna tell my Kai that when I bring this one in. Oh yes. I rub my palms and wince. The bloody palm isn't healing, and I can't stand it. Apprehension that I might be in presence of divinity makes me itchy. I scratch my back on the rock behind me.

The pod door pops open, and the first thing I see is a pointed foot with five toes. I suppress a joyful squeal. I'll squeal plenty with my tribemates as I set up the portal controls for our games. I won't be competing for this female. I'm not even telling them which goddess I think she is or where I got her from. Nobody would compete for the daughter of Herea. I really ought to hand her over to the Ra, let her drink their blood while they wail like terriks during the mating cycle.

A leg extends, and her toes touch the sand. Those are some long, finely shaped legs. Real long. Almost as long as mine, but thinner, prettier, feminine. The other leg joins the first, and then I see hands running up and down the leg, spreading glistening oil over the skin. The movement of her arms, also long and thin, and graceful hands entraps me, and briefly, I imagine those slender hands stroking my abdomen and lower yet.

I fix my erection, shift a little, and crouch, leaning my elbow on the rock that I should be using to hide my position, not as a place for ogling a female who might bleed me for a turn or more if she doesn't have anything else to do. And there's nothing to do out here.

She steps out of the pod and inhales deeply, closes her eyes for a moment. Her golden hair is tightly pulled in a high neat bun, and her face is…well, one of a goddess, meant to be admired and worshiped and lusted over. She's tall, and she's rubbing some kind of oil over her nude body. Although thin, she's strong and curvy at the same time. In fact, her fitness is quite uncanny and unexpected.

And soon I find out why.

The womankind walks away from the pod with her toes pointing forward, then rises on said toes and starts dancing, extending and bending one long leg at the knee while twirling in a fast cycle that makes my head spin. If I had any doubt that the goddess of grace walks the Blood Dunes again, I don't anymore. I'm glued to my position, unable to take my eyes off her or move to snatch her while she's distracted in her dance, leaping from one leg to another, executing splits nobody in our lands can replicate. It's not only the legs. The way her entire body moves gives an impression of a feather swaying on the wind. It's…it's mesmerizing, and I purr as I rise a little more so I can admire her dance.

The breeze picks up her scent and sends it to me. I inhale a lungful, and my balls are so happy, they almost jingle together. She's the most graceful of…prey. I lick my teeth, my gums swelling. Fuck, I'm hungry and horny, and her flesh would satisfy both needs. I knock on my head to be sure I'm not winded. Still something ringing in there, so that's good.

I continue watching from afar. She's so beautiful when she's unaware that anyone is watching. Most prey are, but none provide admirable entertainment like this one.

Hart said womankind don't leap.

He said they're awkwardly uncoordinated.

That's because he's never seen Eme dance. But he will as soon as I bring her in. All there's left for me to do is find her nesting place, open a portal into Kalia, and let her walk through. This is gonna be so easy. Mm-hm... Read more

MEET THE ALPHA BEAST

A SNIPPET FROM BLIND BEAST MATE

J*amie*

I'd almost kidnapped Rey straight out of her home, put her on my bike, and driven her to my house. That was how crazy I'd been when I first saw her smile. For us—the beasts from faraway planet Tineya— mating was a simple process. You saw a female, you felt she was your female, you took the female and made her yours. Making her yours meant conquering her pussy with might, fucking her to oblivion to get her into heat. That was our whole purpose as mated male beasts. To conquer our mate's pussy and get our mates pregnant with little beast babies.

We never told the communities we depended on their females for mating. We couldn't tell them we needed *the* girl and not any girl. We'd told them we took girls as pairs as if we could choose between many, even went as far as buying random women and putting them in the cities. It kept the power in our hands, or they'd try to fuck with us. Or hurt our mates.

Vice—the ass—had lost his mate before he'd even claimed her. We'd been looking for her all over this godforsaken land. We came to Rey's community in search of Vice's mate but found mine instead. I couldn't get Rey out of my mind, and the fact her uncle wouldn't let her talk to us, wouldn't let her join us for lunch, made me want to kidnap her even more.

I didn't ask him to pair her with me the same day. Instead, I'd listened to my brother Vice when he'd advised against mixing with scum the likes of her uncle. He'd said to be certain Rey was mine before asking for her. I went back home and couldn't get a wink of shut-eye all night. What if she ran off like Vice's mate had, and I couldn't find her? Naturally, this idea made me crazy.

Early the next day, I yanked one of their priests out of his bed so he could draw up the pairing papers. I rode back to her community with said papers and a case of money I'd strapped to my bike. Her uncle, the greedy bastard, had taken all of five minutes to sign the papers and take the money, but he held my mate for another week. Motherfucker.

But she was here now. Click!

MILANA'S BACKLIST

Dirty Wolf and Jake are exclusive to my newsletter subscribers
HERE!

Tribes:

Marked #1, Stolen #2, Lured #3

Read the complete Beast Mates Series:

#0 Virgin - FREEBIE, #1 Blind, #2 Wild,

#2.5 Goddess, FREE via my Mailing List,

#3 Sent, #3.5 Their, #4 Caught, #4.5 His, #5 Free.

Read the Complete Horde Series:

#1 Alpha Breeds, #2 Alpha Bonds, #3 Alpha Knots, #4 Alpha Collects

The Complete Hordesmen Series:

Hunger #1, Terror #2, Sidone #3, Fever #4, Dreikx #5, The Blind
Hordesman #6

Read the complete Dragon Brotherhood:

Rise #1, Burn #2, Storm #3, Fight, #4

Short stories in IADB World: Jake 1.5, Eddy #2.5

Read the complete Age of Angels series:

Court of Command, #1 • Court of Sunder, #2 • Court of Virtue, #3

ABOUT THE AUTHOR

Milana Jacks grew up with tales of water fairies that seduced men, vampires that seduced women, and Babaroga who'd come to take her away if she didn't eat her bean soup. She writes sci-fi fantasy romance with dominant monsters from her home on Earth she shares with Mate and their three little beasts.

• Sometimes she releases stories for the readers on her mailing list as they await for books in the series. If you want in, join other readers at http://www. milanajacks.com/newsletter/ •

Meet me at
www.milanajacks.com

Made in the USA
Columbia, SC
23 July 2021

42328848R00093